On Deerback to a Sunset Unknown

On Deerback to a Sunset Unknown

Hrusikesh Panda

Translated from Odia by
Lipipuspa Nayak

BLACK EAGLE BOOKS
Dublin, USA | Bhubaneswar, India

Black Eagle Books
USA address:
7464 Wisdom Lane
Dublin, OH 43016

India address:
E/312, Trident Galaxy, Kalinga Nagar,
Bhubaneswar-751003, Odisha, India

E-mail: info@blackeaglebooks.org
Website: www.blackeaglebooks.org

First International Edition Published by
Black Eagle Books, 2024

ON DEERBACK TO A SUNSET UNKNOWN
by **Hrusikesh Panda**
Translated from Odia by **Lipipuspa Nayak**

Cover & Interior Design: Ezy's Publication

ISBN- 978-1-64560-531-7 (Paperback)
Library of Congress Control Number: 2024934271

Printed in the United States of America

Translator's Note

With my doctoral course in the subject of Translation Studies Translation as an academic-literary activity has stayed with me. As part requirement of my PhD thesis, I had opted to translate *Chatura Binod*, the 17th c Odia prose classic, believed to be the first work of fiction in an Indian language. I registered for my PhD in the late nineties of the last century, and was awarded the degree in 2000. The text I subsequently took up for translation was *Harina Pithire Ajana Suryastaku*, the second novel to be authored by Hrusikesh Panda, without realizing how ambitious a choice that was.

Hrusikesh Panda those days was consolidating as a bright, unconventional creative prose writer, particularly acknowledged in literary circuits for his unusual titles, lyrical idiom, trendsetting structures and themes. The "IAS Topper" tag was an incongruity to the artist in the Odia literary world, though soon the tag blended respectably with the creative oeuvre of this exceptionally gifted writer whose literature complemented his activism of work life. The English translation of *Harina…* had been brought out by a New Delhi based publisher and discussed in academia, though I can't say I was very sure of the quality of my translation. Perhaps why I thought I must do this classic

– which will definitely sit beside world classics – justice with a translation more worthwhile and confident.

Harina... astounds me with every reading. Apparently about the drab, eventless life of protagonist Kunti, a school teacher in countryside India, set against a time following its independence, a life confined to the drudgery of everyday dowdy routine that accentuates even more as Kunti is unmarried, how lucidly and effortlessly the novel concludes in poetry and hope! Kunti's few flimsy romantic relationships do not culminate in a secure familial bond, or help her lead a bearable life. She could think of a refuge in her picturesque ancient village of childhood, Ankamara after resigning from her job, which was not to be; what with the village disappearing into a reservoir of a hydro-electric dam constructed by the government on the land surrounding the village, and the villagers shifted to a new settlement in a barren landscape, amid rocks and boulders put up by the government. This is a subplot of the novel summarizing the uprootedness of Kunti as well as a community. Yet in the narrative it is she who retrieves the fates involved!

To do that Kunti metamorphoses into the enigmatic. That is how she reconciles to the cruel transition of a sylvan world to an alien one. Slowly she seeks company from her old world through the souls of dead people. They visit her in her reminiscences and she feels comforted, and the impersonal settlement does not intimidate her anymore, life is not drab anymore. She begins to acquire powers of prescience and divination. She is now taken as someone with divine power, with the ability to predict people's problems and prescribe the solutions. The narration treads the world of the inscrutable, the realm of the mystique; yet the world around her is real too. She does not believe that she has supernatural powers, but everyone else around her believes that she has. This life continues, till she, tired, exhausted and without a goal to achieve, wishes to leave the physical world. A week of rainfall ensues, during which the barren land around the settlement gets filled up with greens, she becomes smaller and smaller, grows a pair of wings and flies away like a fairy riding a deer which has run into her yard covering long stretches of distances, wearing fatigue, without notice of the villagers. The sun was setting on the horizon then.

This is a remarkable work. With a few highpoints that overtake a critic completely. For one, the ingenuous shades of ecofeminism in the narrative where the protagonist's tale has been entwined with the collective tale of a community, a people who suddenly become rootless. Kunti's uprootedness is not hers alone, it is of a community that has been evicted from their ancestral homeland, with its timeless natural splendor, and are relocated to a faceless government settlement in a barren space. While the problems of the people in the new settlement are real – they are unable to adjust to forced displacement, and to the cold artificial structures which is in contrast to their living experiences in a sylvan shelter of verdant nature and agricultural sustenance, and behave funnily, Kunti is salvaging them with the magical powers she is slowly acquiring (or perhaps she has been born with those powers!). Her transformed persona impacts the settlement which gets invaded with magical energies; an unrelenting spell of downpour continues to bathe the settlement, and greens sprout, grow and envelop the rocky settlement in thick woods (perhaps Kunti takes the cover of the woods to fly away). The settlement with its green cover and suddenly acquired ancience almost reverts back to Ankamara. And a little child from the settlement, howsoever fragile his effort may be, rises up and resists one more displacement of his clan people.

Another major aesthetic attribute of the novel is the manner in which it ends. Like Kunti departing from the settlement as a fairytale character riding on the back of a visitor deer at her will. In an "Afterword" to my first translation of the work, which the author had volunteered to answer the issue of "obscureness" about the novel (the "obscurity" about the novel is also because of its compressed structure, compressing about half a century of social realism into a hundred pages) and which expectedly served as an epilogue, there is this submission of the novelist: 'The sun rises every day, and sets, what a simple fact! So is Kunti's simple life, nothing happens to it as nothing happens to the sun between its rise and setting. No incident, no accident, no splurge, only the sun saunters away leisurely. In a typical story so many things happen, someone drudges away to progeria, someone wastes away with alcohol, someone become rich, someone becomes poor, someone falls ill and someone dies; but look at this poor Kunti, she achieves nothing, arrives nowhere; the pristine moment does not arrive in her life when she could have taken someone in her arms. Yet how poignant and lonely her sunset is? ... The poignancy of a persona like Kunti was captured by poet Ramakanta Rath in one of his earliest poems *Mastrani* (the school mistress) and I quote (translation is mine):

> *Two and two make four;*
>
> *Why should such a simple truth*
>
> *In order to be established*

Consume my entire youth?

Where will I get a story from, how do I construct a plot, how do I describe her life, how do I coat her with vividity? Forgive me dear reader, please, I did not deceive you on purpose, I could not be capable of creating.'

And the narrative recourses to poetic justice. An evolved protagonist is sanctioned powers of the inexplicable as the narration progresses. Hers is now a fairytale life; her uprootedness is now treated with materials of fairytale reality that governs her life. She acquires the ability to forewarn, talk with the dead, forgive the men she had been inclined romantically to, yet which remained unrequited, snap ties with the world so that she can just evaporate without a chord holding her back anywhere; she flies away like a fairy, growing a pair of wings, riding a deer.

On a different plane this aesthetically convincing ending has an allusion in a particular folklore tradition of Odisha where girls are deified in their misfortunes. Kalijai, an adolescent girl is a timeless heroin in the Odia folklore. Kalijai, a young bride in the Chilika lagoon leaving for her in--laws from one island to another in the Chilika lagoon, for the first time after marriage, is caught up in a sudden storm and dies. While her father and others accompanying her survived, she was not found. With years, she becomes a deity in the lagoon who protects the people, boatmen and the fishers; a temple is there in her name inside the lagoon – the Kalijai Temple. Now, why did she become a goddess? She was sad because she was leaving her father's home and going to a stranger's. Most of the girls who get married adjust and carry on with the new life, but perhaps Kalijai was an exception. Her sorrow and tears were unbearable and came in the form of a storm, so goes the collective unconscious, the sorrow that also resulted in her detachment from this world. Such total detachment makes her a goddess detachment leads to "sannyas" and sometimes deity-hood. Kunti's story may be viewed in this classical Indian literary tradition. Most of the discourses on deification are about goddesses, rather than gods. This is part of the feminism inherent in the Indian value and belief systems; an unhappy woman, whom nice experiences remain unrequited, getting elevated to the level of a fairy or a deity, and Odia literature has adequate instances of the reality (*Ta'apoi* is another instance) where the world of real and the mystique and fairytale is indistinguishable.

Kunti's end is migration of the soul too. With her defenselessness in a world that held no lure for her she cannot *die*, she goes through transcendence of the soul. The end of the world for any particular person is indistinguishable from death, and the regeneration following destruction is the image of rebirth too. The novelist says: no one dies in a village; the soul migrates from one form to another. The transition of the protagonist from someone living banal everyday realities to her end in the tradition of Indian belief systems is seamless, the magical blends with the real effortlessly, which is there right from the beginning of the novel. And the consequent positivism in which the novel ends despite the cruelty of events carried.

This powerful work, of about a hundred and twenty pages, is a compact lyrical narrative, with a tight structure that blends worlds of fairytales with social reality of the Earth. The language of the novel is sheer poetry, and like poetry is sensitive to multiple interpretations and impressions. The idiom in its lyricism and quaint colloquiality is extremely difficult, challenging easy translation. Only, I have tried to get closer to the original.

Harina... is the second book by the novelist. It connects thematically to both its predecessor *Shun Sange Samayika Sandhi* (a temporary truce with zero) and successor *Sunaputra Loke* (*The People of Sunaput*). While the first book discusses absurdity of existence and meaninglessness of life through the life's story of an unemployed youth, handled with humour, *Sunaput...* takes up repeated government sponsored displacements of a forest and hill community of southern Odisha on a larger scale and the subsequent uprising of a violent movement. The author has often expressed that he was unsure about his career as a writer, and his readership. *Sunaput...* brought him the prestigious Bhubaneswar Book Fair Award (1992), dispelling irreversibly any such cynicism.

Lipipuspa Nayak

ONE

Nearly everyone in that small town, said to be of the size of a ludo board, knew that Bhanu will finally marry the hospital nurse Enigma, that is, everyone except Kunti, a school teacher and Bhanu's beloved. It was a holiday. Kunti had finished cooking lunch early, covered the dishes with lids, gazed at the ceiling, and was restive; she slept off and then woke up in many cycles. Her room had a small veranda on the front. She had, in real, rented a small part of the giant-sized house of an enormous north-Indian trader. Her bedroom, kitchen, bath and toilet had crowded together on the front side of the main structure of the building. After her room, there was a well in the courtyard. The entrance to the house was after the well, a front door humbles like a door to a backyard.

The coalesced tranquility of an entire afternoon. Except the wind sighing occasionally through a thick and leafy peepul tree. The road outside cannot be seen from the house, the noise from the road can hardly be heard. A day of strange and absolute solitude, though solitude does not stun Kunti these days at all. It was such a day, like in a monsoonal Ashadha month, the torrential rain ceases in the morning suddenly, the low-hanging clouds disappear slowly and completely from the sky, refulgent sunshine reigns through the day, and the blazing sunshine will throw a question bluntly to your face that could burn your face, and so Kunti is scurrying back into her house out of fear.

She had thought with so much earnestness yesterday that she would surely spend the Sunday sleeping! Now as she rolls on the bed, the bed is sticky with her sweat. The moment her eyelids closed, she was travelling by a bus through a very big town; she got down to buy something she cannot remember and she had a growing terrible thirst. She went near a drinking water point and found a long queue of thirsty people there. Her rainbow coloured crystal glass was smashed into smithereens in the scramble as thirsty people pushed and elbowed each other to rush ahead. The aggressive, merciless people wearing faces of unconcern, and amid them Kunti fell asleep, there, on the ground.

When she woke up, her body had an excitement of distrust. People thronged around her, everywhere, yet no one had a face. There was a pervasive clamor everywhere, but in the language of animals and birds of some mythological forest. Kunti's illusory sleep was dissipated. She felt someone outside was calling her by her name, though she felt like this often and no one really came for her. Yet she came out of her room.

Outside it was a shameless wild sunshine, like a tiger, who asked to her face in loud bursts: 'So, one more day of yours is wasting away? What are you doing about it?'

With her habitual obstinacy (which she had preserved so cautiously all along, as though if she let go of it she would be left with nothing) she said: 'Why? It is full! I have to wash clothes, got to reply to uncle Govind's letter. It's fine with me if uncle has written to me to find out about his son's exam scores, and granted that I have not found out on that; does that mean I can't write to him asking after his health or illness?'

She continued to argue with herself: "Would he not be willing to know how I am doing here? Besides, Tandra has sent me a card. She has a beautiful name, *Tandra – dreamy*, my student, and the card is her brother's wedding invite. Does that mean I wouldn't even reply to her? Tomorrow I must pull up that class teacher of grade Seven. How strange it is that that her name skips me! She is late every day. The students roam in the meadows; one or two guardians have lodged complaints already. Of course, guardians are guardians; they lodge complaints anytime anyway; in fact, they *have* to lodge complaints".

Kunti, in the same belligerent pose, wound her sari end firmly around her waist and went to the kitchen. She took out the utensils and plates and quarter plates and quarter bowls and spoons and ladles, and washed them again. She collected the washed clothes from the clothes rack and folded some into a neat column and kept aside the rest for ironing. Only then she noticed that there was no electricity. She took out audio cassettes and the player from the steel cupboard to play, and again noticed that there was no electricity. So, she dusted the cassette player, wrapped it in an embroidered cotton length and put it back, and despite all these chores a quarter of the afternoon was still left over. An abrupt fatigue overwhelmed her. She fetched the snacks jar, fished out fistfuls of snacks of puffed rice and oil fried green grams and groundnuts with spices which had chili powder from the jar and munched on it. The snacks gave her a feeling of irritation, yet she did not stop at munching the spicy stuff. At the end her lips burned suddenly, her gums pained and her stomach belched up sour liquid. She popped an antacid pill and fell asleep.

As soon as she closed her eyes, she saw a place; the place looked familiar to her. With a little thought she remembered that once, while travelling in a bus, two passengers were talking and as the bus was entering the city limits they pointed at the place and remarked: a cremation ground. She had looked out then and had not found any signs of a cremation ground there. There was a storm water drain flowing by near the place, but she did not find broken pieces of clay pots or a burning pyre or a jackal anywhere. But as she looked on, suddenly something like a logogram of small grasses sprouted there all over with a sputtering sound, like mushroom, and filled up the place. *What is it?* Kunti fretted, confused, her stomach cramped and churned. She remembered in a while a certain childhood scene: she had been little and was peeping at the village map as senior villagers were reading the map and discussing something very seriously. She had seen this "logogram" there. At the bottom of the map in the endnotes, there was an explanation of all the signs in the map, and there was this sign with the remarks "Village Cremation Ground".

Kunti opened her eyes. In the afternoon sky a few absent-minded clouds were floating. In the wind, the usual feeling: hey-something-I-have-lost-something-I-don't-know-I-have-lost-come-on-I-lost-something-you-see.

There, leaning against a wooden post on the veranda, the post is among the ones supporting the tin-sheet roof, Kunti is not ready to admit that she has been waiting for someone; yet her face is flustered, her heart is restive and fluttered. Is her elder brother keeping well? He hasn't written to her for a year now. No, it will be a little less than a year. She had sent a *rakshi* for him during the festival time, praying for his safety, and he had sent her a return gift of fifty rupees by postal money order, with the message on the coupon that Kunti's sister-in-law (that is his wife) was not in good health, she had endless migraine. So it was just a case of migraine, why should anything worse happen to them? Someone knocked on the entrance from outside! Is that a telegram, Kunti panicked. Is sister-in-law no more? Or is brother serious? Kunti is arranging her sari in a hurry, the hook of the blouse does not fasten. She is rushing to open the door for the khaki-clad postman and lo, a woman, dark-complexioned, an oversized nose ring on the septum and a bun on one side of her head is asking: 'Will you buy some flattened rice, ma?'

Kunti chased the vendor woman and turned back. The granddaughter of her house owner, her hair held in an elastic band topped with a white plastic butterfly, had drawn flower murals on the ground. As soon as she saw Kunti, she asked: 'Will you be my grandmother? Today my prince is due to come.'

Two or four speeding knives swished through Kunti's brain. She looked everywhere around, walked to the girl and asked: 'You have a grandmother, don't you?'

'Yes, but she is totally useless. She doesn't understand what I say.'

Kunti whispered into her ear: 'That's okay; but do I look like your grandma? Why did you ask me to be your grandma?'

'What can I do then?' the girl said. 'The story needs this. I will have decorated the ground with flowers before the arrival of my prince. The prince will come and ask, little girl, dear little girl, have you done the flowers; little girl, dear little girl, will you be my empress?'

Kunti returned to her house and opened the door of her room, the muddy shoe marks of the postman, who had brought the news that someone who was supposed to come will never come, had daubed the walls, steel cupboard, ceiling of the room, tube light, suitcase, bed, blades of the ceiling fan and the back of the dial of her wrist watch which she had kept upturned. The moment she opened the cupboard, a cupboard-full of sorrow tumbled down: someone was supposed to come, yet will not. She upturned the rice pot that had been kept with its open side to the ground because the water had drained off. Some amazing and exotic occurrence, something esoteric, was to happen, but it did not happen only because of her utter absence of trust and confidence in herself.

Kunti got up and closed the door of the room with sufficient noise, so that the house owner heard it; she moved the cleat of the door with a clatter as if she was hooking it, but left it unhooked and flung herself on the bed, and waited for Bhanu.

Rain began to fall in big, isolated drops. From the sound she can distinctly recognize the kind of pattering raindrops on a tin sheet somewhere! From which direction is the sound coming in? Today perhaps Bhanu will not come. Bhanu, of course, comes to Kunti stealthily, as quietly as a thief. If he has to come during daytime, he comes holding a packet of sweetmeat wrapped in sal leaves, and talking and screaming in a loud voice – that suits his personality of a football player.

Bhanu came eventually, imperceptibly, though Kunti did not know how much time had passed by since she had been waiting for him. Drenched in a drizzle, his bald patch winked sparsely from his wet hair. He sneaked into the house, closed the entrance door from inside and went into Kunti's room. The house owner who had kept the door and windows of his room open and was watching from upstairs, pretended that he did not see anything, and prostrated on the floor to cock his ears to it. As either his grandson or granddaughter defecated on the veranda of his house he grumbled with irritation; because they were getting late for the evening show, this film was tax-free, the film that will come after this one will perhaps be a box-office hit and he cannot afford to watch that film in the theatre along with his entire family.

Kunti opened her eyes, got up silently, sat up on the bed quietly and said: 'Pssst!'

As Bhanu went and sat by her on the bed, Kunti was shocked to see how his hair had thinned on his scalp and said: 'Wait, let me go and check.'

She served food for Bhanu hastily. Bhanu was not hungry; he asked Kunti if she would not eat lunch. Like every other time, this time too, Kunti told him the lie that she had finished lunch. (Every Sunday, throughout the day, Kunti goes without a grain of food, in a way waiting for Bhanu, as if as part of an austere holy ritual. Or is it to atone for the sin about their relationship?) Bhanu thought that with this meal he would save from his dinner about an average ten rupees, and gulped the food. Besides, rice served in a restaurant has stones and soda in it, the curry is cooked with oil not of mustard seed, but that came from the juice of a toxic wild fruit, and with rotten vegetables, and the water they use for cooking has sulphate like salts which damage the liver – some such idea Bhanu had been carrying from his childhood days. Therefore, though he was compelled to eat food at shanty like shops, he had a terrible discomfort about it. He sulked silently that Kunti did not wait for him for lunch. But he did not articulate anything aloud and finished the food in rapid gulps.

Kunti was lazing on the bed by the time Bhanu finished. Bhanu washed his hand there in the plate and kept sitting there by the plate, on the doormat. He pulled out strands of coir from the mat, rolled it into a lump and chewed the lump mindlessly.

The empty stomach of teacher Kunti secreted hydrochloric acid and grated and churned, and she said 'my stomach is aching' and rolled on the bed again, waiting: Bhanu would get up and in a gesture of touch-me-touch-me-not caress her belly!

Bhanu continued to squat where he was, and he was wondering how to break the news of his proposed marriage before Kunti. The doormat was new, it was not yielding much coir thread. Kunti lifted her face, rested on her elbow and spoke with a reddened face: 'Did you come here to sit there, on that doormat?'

Bhanu is remembering a chameleon, in particular the chameleon's chin. On Bhanu's lean bachelor's face, his teeth that looked so pretty earlier, now look dirty and crooked, stained from chewing betel cones.

Kunti got down from the cot and pulled Bhanu by the hand. '*Arey*, don't get angry my dear.' She is unable to pull him and says: 'Well, get angry with me as much as you can and be happy.'

Kunti looks utterly skinny, her veins show up. Somewhere somebody drops some bronze utensils to the floor.

Bhanu shudders and says: 'Your mouth is smelling.'

'I don't eat fish, meat, egg, raw onion, yet why did he say that?' Kunti thinks and is looking for her toothbrush hurriedly. She is fidgety, she can't find her toothbrush. She fetches edible salt, mustard oil and charcoal, mixes them and brushes her teeth with the mixture with her index finger. After brushing she sits on the bed, caresses Bhanu's hand, shudders with some inscrutable imaginary fear and looks out through the window, gets down, opens the door, takes the plate Bhanu had eaten from to the kitchen and keeps it for wash, returns to the room, keeps the door ajar, kisses Bhanu briefly and goes out of the room again. There is a nasty boisterous clamour outside.

The house owner ambulated out for the evening film show; his wife, grandchildren, servant and cat trailing behind him. 'What movie is running,' asks Kunti in her faltering Hindi.

'Do keep an eye on the house,' the house owner replies.

Bhanu was listening to the conversation; he rushed out of the room. Sweat beads accumulated on his forehead. 'Close the door, the entrance door,' he says. Kunti is standing on the circular parapet of the well, a coir rope in her hand, a metal bucket tied to the tip of the rope and a sharp and excited question on the tip of her tongue ready to dart out; a question like a clown in a circus who holds his ground firmly with gravitas despite his endless humiliation.

Kunti thinks: 'What does Bhanu want? It cannot be me!'

The yoked bucket is rattling on the inner wall of the well.

Bhanu returned to the room and was waiting for Kunti. Two men returning from the market are heard talking loudly. On the road, the main road, the full-throated haunting cry of someone, who had been left behind in the market, was tearing through the silence and solitude of the night: *'Dina bhai lo, ho dear brother Dina, it is getting dark...'* The echo reverberated and returned unanswered, the eerie yowl intensified: *Dina bhai lo, ho dear brother, it's getting dark, dear...*

Cloyed and soaked in an unexpected intense empathy, Bhanu thought: 'How I wish I were his Dina bhai!'

Bhanu has forgotten about Kunti completely though he is lazing on her bed. The rattle of the bucket is shattering the pervading silence. A song is rising from the bottom of the well and is slipping into the slender-necked brass water-pot like a little dance loving female imp! Thereafter, the footsteps of Kunti. And then the power goes off.

'Can't she come now?' Bhanu wishes.

Kunti, after filling all the buckets, has waited outside, as if the merciless god will write a merciless annual confidential career report for her if she comes to the room and touches Bhanu even so lightly in that translucence. The lights return and reflect between stretches of purple and violet blossoms of water-hyacinth in the pond outside the window.

Kunti now returned to the room. In the street light leaking through the window, she looks tinier and fragile and falls loosely from the agitated hands of Bhanu. She grows restless, disengages herself and goes to the door to open it. An indescribable fear silences her interior – the fear that has been familiar to her since her childhood: during the rains, endlessly dripping through ominous darkness, the frogs croaked; on one side of the village a pregnant river overflowed its banks to inundate and devastate the hills and jungles of her village. On the other side where the forests are, and from that far side terrifying wild animals swooped down in her imagination.

Bhanu is exhausted and withdraws into the solitude inside him; Kunti runs after him and entreats: Are you upset with me dear Kanhu, my little god Krishna, my Bhanu dear?'

Meanwhile, Bhanu is confronting himself: 'Where had I come, and why? With what hope? Don't I know that Kunti, with assault from innumerable imaginary sexual experiences, is now exhausted and lying drained out?'

Kunti is prattling some nonsense rapidly and incessantly as if the moment she stops, Bhanu will vanish mysteriously. Bhanu has gazed at the street, through the window, glancing past the darkness over the water-hyacinth and water-lettuce weeds. A bus stands there under a tube-light, a man in a blue shirt (a blue colour so common in hair salons) is arranging stacks of banana bunches on the roof of the bus. Beyond the bus is a wood cabin, half of which has disappeared below the street. At a distance, the sound of a train is tooting away *chhuk... chhuk...*

'My life is emptied out here,' Bhanu thought. 'All my love I spent here was dissipated like moisture in a desert; what do I have left over for Enigma?' An angered hopelessness shrouded his mind.

Meanwhile, Kunti made rounds of the veranda

again and again, to check if anyone was there outside eavesdropping, came back, ran her fingers through Bhanu's hair, pressed his palm, implored him to smile, and went out again and again. She told Bhanu that she has been thinking every moment of him, throughout the day till he arrived, as on every other day, and begged him to be not so rude, as his rudeness hurt.

Three unruly students of class Ten came to her house in the pretext of getting some lessons explained to them, saw Bhanu there and exchanged naughty signs. Bhanu was even more peeved and sat silently in a corner.

On their return the girls lingered around with the boyfriend of one of them for some time, and resolved unanimously that once they reached home they would tell their folk that the teacher had a guest and hence they were delayed.

One more hour has passed by; one more hour from the quota of life that Bhanu would have spent with Kunti.

A thin, titillating breeze wafted in. Perhaps in another place, not so far away, where there was no sorrow, where an eventless day, even an eventless object like a rock atop a snow-capped mountain cliff was impossible to imagine, even over there the ancient rain had already arrived carrying with it some of its passionate dexterity. At that very moment, when the breeze had just begun to drift out, Kunti told Bhanu about the cramps in her lower abdomen, the ache in her head, and about the wedding of Tandra's brother. She rolled in peals of laughter as she narrated how the brother was marrying from a different caste and if it would not make into a lovely popular gossip.

She also narrated how another day when she was

returning from the education inspector's office, a man chased her cycle-rickshaw for quite a distance, and then she came across a group of people, among them the loafer son of her school Secretary, and got down from the rickshaw hoping desperately that he would rescue her from the stalker. She went to the loafer son, requested him to escort her to her house. Just then it came back to her – the words of the wife of her second brother, who years ago had told to her face – *love of a friend or an acquaintance lasts only for a couple days, unlike a son's or a husband's; an acquaintance cannot be a husband*. And as though a plain literal mention of the message would not have been painful enough, the sister-in-law had said this through a bantering adage. It had been ages since she had said this, but Kunti has not forgotten; she broke into loud tears and told Bhanu she has been having terrifying dreams every night, the details of the dreams could vary but the crux of them is like this: she has been to a new place, on transfer or picnic, or after having died, or while travelling to her village one day, for some obscure reason her bus went off to an altogether new place, or perhaps was hijacked away by some unknown mercenaries or terrorists to some unknown land, and so on. In all these dreams she was marooned in some strange place, in dense woods, or on an islet big enough to hold her two feet only, and inside the tiny islet is a lake, huge like a sea. Or on another day she was swinging – she was little – and the swing goes up, up, up and she reaches the sky, she is there on a cold awful cloud of the colour of over-burnt clay pitcher, and the cloud is about to melt. She is all alone in that expanding void. The dream would not have shattered her if someone's loving arms had gathered her when she woke up from sleep bathed in fear. But there would be no one. A few mosquitoes would be humming inside the netting, or away at a distance an inauspicious nocturnal bird would be hooting intermittently. Every bird twitter nowadays sounds to her like hoots of an owl, a forewarning of death and calamity.

The afternoons do not trouble her; they glide by with school hours. What all refuse to pass are the apathetic mornings, the desiccated and sad evenings and the intimidating stifling nights, oppressive, lonely. Go on to gaze at the sky, think of this acquaintance, that friend. Spare a thought for god, against whom she has such a heap of grievances, that she refuses to acknowledge him at times. Such times descend heavily on her, but what magic is it that the time she keeps busy flies away, like the moments spent with Bhanu, but after his departure lingers on with everlasting remnants of time! And the moments that do not spend themselves, the colourless, odourless and tasteless boredom of which permeates her blood, nervous system, red blood corpuscles and atoms and molecules and quarks of her body do not leave behind any residue at all after they die away!

'What would Enigma be doing now?' Bhanu thought. Soon his thoughts moved to the football match that was coming; he must be the skipper of the sub-district soccer team this time for the league-match. His face began to glow at this prospect, when Kunti said: 'Do I know why you come to me? Yes, I do. I know that you do not love me, you have no affection for me, you come for that; but remember if something happens to me can I show my disgraced face to anyone? Suppose I lose my job for this unwed motherhood, will you shelter me with you? I know you will not...'

Bhanu is miserable and anxious to break the news of his marriage. Kunti pinched his lower lip. Somewhere a cow swished away something; Kunti shuddered and went out to check.

Bhanu is upset and gets up to leave. A second phase of cajoling and supplications. Some teardrops. A few love-pecks. Bhanu settles on the bed again and quickly conveys that if the school secretary agrees, he could be the skipper of the soccer team, and other such things. 'Bhanu *shall* be the skipper' Kunti scribbles on her heart, like it is a slate.

'You do not tell me about football anymore?' Kunti asked.

'What can I tell? Will these league matches take me to the Olympics?'

There is another phase of emotion-choked teardrops and affection.

The house-owner is returning with his family covered in a cloud of noise. A dreadful, eerie night is settling down. It is about nine or half past nine in the evening. How will Kunti explain Bhanu's presence in her house at this hour? Especially when no one will ask her about it in an open conversation?

And at this precise moment a terrible revolt overwhelms Bhanu: 'Why must my presence anywhere be explained to the world?'

Despite the revolting thoughts Bhanu runs the comb through his hair quickly, comes out of the room and slips his feet into the shoes. His shirt has a lumpy dark blotch somewhere on the back and every family member of the house-owner, including their cat, is giggling. He ignores Kunti's cringing whisper: 'Wait, when are you coming again?'

He overlooks the familial brigade of the house-owner and is expelling himself. Kunti is trampling the anger hoisting inside her and mutely blesses Bhanu. She recalls, long ago when she had quit her job at a private school and joined a government school with better job security, and Bhanu's letters were not coming in a long time, she had gone to an astrologer to find Bhanu's whereabouts.

The astrologer had said: 'Of course Bhanu would return, but in another shape. His face would be filled with vulgar acne by then. His body would be stinking of the desire to sleep with dirty and unchaste women. He would linger for a few days, then he would leave you and go away so quietly that nobody would know when he leaves, not even you.'

'Why had I come here?' Bhanu ponders while leaving. 'Habit of an ancient subservience, as a former treasurer or a house manager feels for his former king. What other bonding do I have with teacher Kunti? Am I such a handsome cruel rogue whose heart is just shut out for everything else? Suppose, I go back to Kunti now and tell her clearly: *Look here, I don't love you anymore. Do you remember Enigma, the staff nurse, whose jasmine-laden braids tickled us and whose powder coated face made us ridicule her – my marriage has been fixed with her!* What will happen then? Will she hurl her wood-and-iron kitchen vegetable cutter at me? Or will she go utterly insane and rusticate me from her school? Or else will she just sit there and collapse of a sudden heart attack?'

Bhanu thus decided that he would slowly get out of Kunti's life, imperceptibly, and gently, so gently that even he would not realize his withdrawal. With the decision, a decision he immediately knew was not easy to carry out, he knocked on a door and Enigma, clad in her night-gown, opened it.

By and by, Bhanu faded out from Kunti's life. Kunti had gone to his house a few times after he stopped seeing her. On one occasion Bhanu sent word that he was not home. Another time when she went there and waited in the sitting room, Bhanu sneaked out through the back door and went right away to Kolkata. It dawned on Kunti, eventually, that Bhanu would not come anymore. Still she did not go mad and did not mull over committing suicide. *Every suffering perhaps is an experience* – she solaced herself – *and I must learn from it.*

About five years later she was transferred to Koraput, the southern-most district of the State.

TWO

When Kunti was transferred to Koraput at the southern end of the State in the hills with abounding forests, Sujata, another teacher of the school, said to Kunti: 'Do you know, so-and-so teacher said, why is teacher Kunti so perturbed? Which one of her children or bed-ridden family members is going to be deprived of mother's affection or abandoned to destitution? She should go away presto to wherever she is transferred. What an inhuman person she is! My whole body was on fire. I would have given her a thorough dressing-down, but the rage inside me clasped my mouth shut. I could not utter a word.'

The face, eyeglasses and hairdo of teacher Sujata are such that anyone who looks at her face for a minute is bound to end up giggling. Thus Kunti too broke into a smile. So teacher Sujata's face became pale, she scratched her ears carefully, so that the makeup does not smudge. She returned to the school and whispered into the ears of the Tailoring teacher who was hard of hearing: 'Teacher Kunti has gone bonkers.'

The Tailoring teacher promptly went to everyone she could find in the school and whispered: 'Teacher Kunti is marrying.' (Later, when Kunti resigned from her secure government job, everyone said that she has married and returned to her family in the village.)

When Kunti met the President of the school management committee and with his help the Member of Legislative Assembly from the local constituency and requested for cancellation of her transfer to the other end of the State, her face burnt in the crowd of visitors who had come with their requests. She remembered her father, brothers, mother and Bhanu and was choked with unshed tears. She blamed her mother the most like every other time when she brimmed with unshed tears. The Hon'ble member of the legislative assembly had been elected for the first time recently. He was thrilled with pleasure because Kunti had *approached* him and he smiled a gentle intermittent smile. His face had accumulated some fat which made his eyes smaller. In spite of all her worries, a smile appeared on Kunti's face which she hid under a corner of her sari. The Hon'ble member listened with his eyes closed to everything Kunti said, lighted a cigarette, and wrote down Kunti's name on a paper. He misspelt her name (In government papers, there are such inevitable mistakes, Kunti thought), Kunti bent down and corrected the wrong spelling of her name, and when she straightened, there was a mild pain from her hemorrhoids. Even a year after this, when she had bleeding from this part of her body and was worried about irregular menstrual bleeding, she did not know that she had hemorrhoids.

Kunti and the President of the school management committee came out. Kunti asked about the expenses for her work. The President said: 'Later.' After they had walked some more distance, the President said: 'I will check about the expenses and let you know later.' The same evening the President sent a message for the expenses, and the next day Kunti drew money from her bank account and paid this to the President in his hands.

Since that day there were rumours about her transfer everyday: she will have to go, she will not go, the transfer has been cancelled, no not cancelled, yes cancelled, no, yes... These rumours made Kunti so uncertain and confused that she hung like Trishanku of *Mahabharata,* halfway between earth and heaven. When the uncertainty and confusion began to be painful, she decided to go to Koraput and gathered some geographic, economic and social information about the place.

The general knowledge she gathered included: it rains heavily in Koraput, but it does not rain everywhere in Koraput, this means that there are places where snow falls in winter, no snow does not actually fall but it is as cold as snowfall, in most schools the number of children is less than the number of teachers. Women keep the upper part of their body uncovered, a woman has five or six husbands and the name and conjugal right of each husband is according to the day of the week. Bears dance on the roads in daytime and tigers knock on the backdoor in nights begging for the sour water of watered-rice. Koraput is otherwise known as Kalapani or Andaman island (the place where accused persons of India under trial sentenced to life imprisonment were incarcerated during British rule) of Odisha because someone who went there on transfer did not return to the plains during his service career.

On the other part of her world, inside and outside the school, she carried the burden of unsolicited rodomontade and arrogance of pretentiously helpful people, and the burden grew into a severe inferiority complex inside her. She feigned to respect the braggartism about getting her transfer cancelled of the loafing and good-for-nothing son of the Secretary of the school management committee.

Another round of disgracing rumours calumniated about her. Her habit of breaking into momentary tears over small things returned, a habit she had got rid of with a lot of effort some years ago. Bhanu did not come to her anymore, and she had become sure that, as the astrologer had forecast, he will not come anymore. Yet, she had a feeling, a not so infrequent feeling that Bhanu will return surely and beg for her forgiveness.

One Mayadhar who appeared like a charlatan and demon (he came as a professional witness in various court cases, had his lunch at Kunti's place and saved some money from the expenses paid by the litigant for whom he came as a witness) appeared to be a kin and friend now. Kunti made him stay until the time of the last bus, and after Mayadhar left, cried with real emotion.

She tolerated the arrogance of teacher Uma, the most cantankerous person in the school, with indulgence and affection.

The compensation granted by the government for the irrigation project had been received some days ago, and her family members had not come to her thereafter, for quite some time. She had no news of her family members. Even Gobara, her youngest sibling, who was in Assam did not write to her regularly and when he wrote, the letters had no news.

One day she learnt from newspapers that Govind had become a minister of the government. Her doubt as to whether he was her Govind, despite the brief, exaggerated and flattering news and a young man's photograph. was cleared away. She thought: 'Yes, he is in politics, there would be no dearth of good food and healthy air for him, why should he not remain young?'

Kunti thought and she had an intuitive feeling that Govind will somehow have a premonition that she is in trouble and come to her. After all ministers get to know everything, she believed. She thought: 'I am an honest woman with scruples and values, how can I approach Govind with a petty issue like my transfer?' This will not be a pretty thing to do. And she was proud: whatever it be, Govind became a minister. She was afraid: such great people will escape the grasp of common people like us and disappear. And she was wondering: do they use toilet like ordinary people? The last question appeared vulgar to her and made her blush and smile.

* * * * *

Many days ago, when Kunti had completed twelve years of age and was running thirteen, Govind had disappeared. She had written to him like she used to, but now no reply came. Nathu said that there is a social revolution in the whole country. (Nathu had said social mutiny, and not revolution, because he was a simpleton who had not studied history in school and did not know the difference between revolution and mutiny.) The mutineers had burnt post offices. When Kunti went to school, she saw that the post office was intact and was working. Nathu explained: 'No. No, not here. Silly girl, our post office is such an ordinary one that no one will look at it as something worth burning down.'

Later a mail compartment attached to a passenger train was washed away by flood water flowing over the rails. Some small plates joining the rails had been removed by revolutionaries. A prestigious rumour spread around that Govind was among the revolutionaries.

Meanwhile, the postmaster's eyes became bad, his

vision was affected, and letters were delivered to wrong persons. Naughty children picked up some letters of Kunti and composed ditties describing her as a girl who had lost her character and who had given a bad name to their clan. Kunti felt disgraced and decided to commit suicide by jumping into the roadside storm water channel. When she returned from school, she stopped there and cried, but when evening came she was scared by the ghosts and returned home.

One day during sports-break at noon in the school, most of the girls and an effeminate boy were going to the post office, they stopped at the betel shop in front of the post office to watch an elephant eat coconut, when Kunti slipped out, went to the post office, and gave the letter (she was not sure of the address) with the cost of postage plus two coins worth one eighth of a rupee as tip to a post peon. But she did not receive any reply to this letter.

Another day she came out of the school on the pretext of watching a monkey dance shown by a juggler, went to the post office and asked the post peon. The post peon looked at her with a sad face, let out a long sad sigh, but could not give any information about Govind.

Some months later, when Kunti was thirteen years one month old, Govind had come to her village. The movement for settling the land taken on rent by sharecroppers from people who had land and who could not cultivate the land was called sharecroppers' movement. At this time, this movement was at its peak. Govind had suddenly become surprisingly tall. He was wearing spectacles. His cheeks were covered with tender short beard, and droplets of sweat hung to the beard. He delivered a speech on the village road hugged by houses on both sides, he put his hands in the pockets of his *fatei*, the Indian bush shirt.

Kunti left her veranda, sat on the veranda of Mahadev Mahalinga facing Govind and asked with her eyes: 'Why did you leave me and go away? What was my fault? I would not have become a burden for you! I was not so incapable, so ugly! Now tell me the truth today, why have you returned today? Have you come back for the sharecroppers' movement, or have you returned to me?'

The time to get ready for school came and Kunti was getting late. Her mother came and called her, Kunti did not listen. The time to leave for school passed; Govind did not leave any impression that he ever knew Kunti and went to the paddy fields where the action for sharecroppers was taking place. Some information trickled in that police was on the way, and half of the men duly scared went away to other villages, their relations in other villages or hid on the inner roof of the house which was made of timber and which was used for storage of fresh fruits and vegetables and for sleeping in summer heat.

Kunti did not go to school on the pretext of disturbances in the village. Mother, whose job was to know everything, understand everything and not say much, did not say anything worthwhile. In the disturbance in paddy field, there was not much physical violence. From behind the crowd, Kunti saw that Govind was felled by the crowd with just two slaps on his cheeks. Kunti tried to run and hold Govind and call him "my love, my love"; but nothing happened. Four young men of the village with bulging muscles picked him up (Govinda looked like a dead chicken) each one holding a hand or a leg and brought him to the village and put him on the village street. The village policeman went to the police station to lodge the information.

Kunti's father was not a village landlord with administrative powers. But her maternal grandfather was a small landlord over a couple of villages and her mother had the temperament of a landlord. Her mother entered through the crowd, reached Govind, administered some medicinal salt, and chastened the villagers: 'You are trying to kill him, or what?'

Some people came towards her and said: 'Look, this is a matter for the police station now, do not get into this. Otherwise do not blame us later.'

Kunti's mother said: 'What police matter are you showing me, you tiny boy with wet pants? If I squeeze your cheeks, milk will come out.'

In the night, Govind slept in the barn house of Kunti's family. Kunti went to him and returned soon after. The memory of her painful humiliation dwarfed her for a long time and until the death of Govind she could not unshackle herself from that memory. In the night police came and took Govind away.

At that time Kunti was dreaming: in the faint twilight she was in the big garden of the village, the thick foliage of taller trees was heavy with darkness and she could not see clearly Govind's face. A group of girls were returning from the darkness of the garden, a river was flowing on the other side of the garden. Kunti was standing on the bank of the river. The girls went away. Kunti stayed behind, hiding quietly. Govind was standing on the dry sand bed of the river, smiling. Kunti kept saying no, no, no and to make the no even more explicit, she slipped along the sandy bank to the river bed. The sand was smooth and slipped down with a soft sound. Her body slipped on the sand, coyness and accompanying clothes separated away from her body, a fire was burning on the sand bed, in every stream of the river injured red-crowned herons wailed. But the air, heavy with emotion, refused to carry the wailing. Kunti was squatting, wet and her chin placed on her knees. Under the moonlight the man was smiling.

Kunti asked: 'Shall I squat like this forever?'

Govind said: 'Queen, my queen, let us run away to somewhere far, very far.'

They tiptoed away on the riverbed alongside the edge, pretending that the edge was the wall of the river, hopping over picturesque river shells, colourful flowers and shining white fishes. Suddenly Kunti grew up, she became a mother and a grandmother, and fought with the whole world over a tiny issue of her son. She loved and hated her husband over nails, toilet, smell of the head, income, gold jewellery, a new shirt. She had a silent affair inside her mind with someone which she lost to utter frustration and returned to her family, vested her last hopes and faith on her sons and daughters, loved her grandsons a little more and granddaughters a little less, clutching on to another round of false hopes and beliefs, became a person with sagged breasts, yellow teeth and hollow cheeks.

Her son wrote to her: 'Ma, with three different places of stay, the expenses are too high and I cannot manage, you better come over here. (If you come over here, the maid servant can come once a day instead of twice).'

When Kunti woke up from sleep, morning had not arrived, and the sky was of electric blue colour. She ran to the house of Sundari. Sundari was whimpering pitiably shedding silent tears. In the night police had come, arrested Govind and took him away. Aha, Kunti did not know and will not know till the last day of her life that in the previous evening after Kunti had returned dejected from Govind, Sundari had slept with him. She will also not know through her life that, the father of her dear friend Dami from class six to ten was murdered. (One night when everyone else in Dami's house had gone somewhere, Kunti had stayed in her house as requested by Dami's family. The two girls slept on the same bed, and in the night, they had taken off their clothes for fear of a ghost, as ghosts did not come near girls without clothes. They hugged each other and slept. They hated all the boys in the school.) Dami's father was the Tahsildar, the Land Officer and Magistrate of a large area. One night, when he had gone to the Annual Day function of the school and was sitting with the audience in the dark open space, someone hit him with a stick or rod and he died on the spot. The murderer was never arrested and no one knew the cause of the murder. Kunti will never know that the murderer was Govind.

Kunti did not cry for Govind then. She hoped for a letter from Govind every day, a letter that did not come. Nathu said: 'Govind had really come to meet Kunti. Otherwise Ankamara is such an insignificant and small village, where there is not even a real sharecropper, that a busy leader like Govind would not rush here for the sake of sharecroppers movement'. What all shattered inside her in those days when the flowers woven on her sari gave out the fragrance of mahwa and other wild flowers. If she raised her eyes, even the hum of bumblebee became silent. Kunti had a fair glistening body, shining and slim. After Govind left, she stopped growing somehow, she looked smaller, she remained small like a child. On the bed, in the courtyard, kitchen, the pond in backyard, the common village lakelet, water lettuce weeds floating in the pond water, tiny coconuts falling down without growing, in the crowds of girls and women returning from the river with full water pitchers on their waists, the cranky father of Markand returning in the night singing out of tune songs, the bouts of rage of the village landlord, the absence of the female cat for half a day, in the retreat of an absent-minded stranger washing his feet in the village pond crumpling its tranquil surface – all around, all the time, the pathos was ancient, like the tunes of flute of Krishna pining for Sri Radha, or the sad lonely ululation of Ta'apoi, the sister of sea-farers waiting for her brothers alone on the seashore, and the pathos was so primordial that it denied her even a drop of tear.

This departure of Govind was the last she saw him for a long time. Kunti received occasional news of him only through numerous rumours: he became an occasional tout, he became president of some cooperative society, he was member of some committees or other in the area, he became the leader for several public causes from time to time, he was elected the president of local self government a couple of times, and that he even specialized as a witness in court cases relating to assault on young women and girls.

There were also chains of gossips which reached Kunti through whispers. He had lost consciousness during a scuffle. He slapped a landlord or businessman in a public place who was dealing with grains and forest produce, who had rented out his building in Cuttack town to prostitutes and who is a terror in a large part of the district and has disappeared. Govind is living with a school teacher, but they are not married; his wife is suffering from cancer after six childbirths; he is suffering from high blood pressure or had a heart attack or both; he has thrown out his father from their house; he has built a hotel at the state capital Bhubaneswar and named it after his daughter who died at the age of three and so on.

The court cases relating to sharecropper movement lingered for a long time without any decision. The land officers and lawyers became richer. Land owners and share-croppers became smart and learnt to maintain paper work so that they do not fail next time another movement starts. But this smartness did not benefit anyone; eventually the movement limped and collapsed. After a few years, the land was submerged under dam water.

* * * * * *

Kunti is trying to find the exact reason of why Govind did not come again and is unable to find a conclusive answer. *Kings. ministers and saints can know everything. How is it possible that Govind did not know about my transfer? The moment he catches a glimpse of me, will he get down like Tarzan from his tusker and like him escort and carry me? Or with the hubris of his throne, he will refuse to acknowledge our relationship completely. And, can I ask him that question now: why he had not come for such a long time, and when he came in the name of sharecropper movement, why he had sent me away with such disdain?*

She decided to go and look up Govind and after taking this decision became indifferent to her situation of whether she will go to Koraput or not. On the other hand, she thought of asking the above question to Govind and the excitement of the thought uplifted her to a transcendent state.

She decided to go in the morning and return in the evening, and therefore, went by an express bus. The driver drove rashly, played the horn in the same rhythm as the speed, turned back to make funny conversation with the passengers without slowing the bus, stared outside at women bathing in roadside ponds, lighted a cigarette with his hands off the steering wheel, and blew the smoke at the signboard "smoking prohibited" inside the bus. Kunti's teacher's heart buzzed to stop such indiscipline, the same teacher's heart showed immediately how disabled she was to enforce any discipline and she dozed off to a slumber.

The bus stopped because a herd of cattle was lazing around the entire width of the road there. Some passengers alighted and pushed the cows and calves gently by their bare hands without using any stick and cleared the road. Kunti woke up and looked at the cattle. She saw a couple of street dogs lazing among the cattle. She told the woman sitting to her left: 'Look at the smart dogs, how they are hiding themselves.'

The woman silenced Kunti with a look as if her eyes were covered with snow and checked to see if her bags and suitcase were in place.

The bus reached the state capital without any accident. As Kunti got down from the bus, she saw a goat trying to overtake an Ambassador brand car which was overtaking a push-cart and almost hit a scooter, (as an empty large truck was overtaking the car at this moment); but the goat escaped miraculously from all this scary melee unhurt and unconcerned, went to the kerb and browsed the grass on the kerb. The passengers were arguing about something when the bus stopped, and now the argument had become loud and aggressive. Like all big and small arguments, they did not arrive at any conclusion. The saint-like grace and quietude of the goat amazed Kunti because in their village, even the little goat-herd girl, let alone the goats, looked so vulnerable and tiny in her three feet long sari.

There was a large crowd waiting in the veranda of Govind's house and the garden in front, and some of them went into the house and came out effortlessly looking awfully busy and important. A constable was chewing betel cone and talking to the visitors affably. The gardener, holding a hose pipe spurting water, was talking to some visitors waving his hands. The water flowed into a storm water drain. There was no grass on the lawn. People sitting on the cement boundary wall, steps, and concrete benches were looking at Kunti with sleepy and mischievous eyes. The odour of sweat from their bodies blew in the memory of her village of several years ago. She thought: *what is this odour, rootless and unfamiliar, doing here?*

'I have come to meet the Minister,' Kunti told some of these people. 'He is my childhood friend.'

'I am personal assistant to the Minister sahib, you sit here and wait,' one of them said. He left.

Another person said: 'No, he is no personal assistant, nor anything. He is just a tout and hanger-on. You wait in this room. The minister is meeting visitors here.' He showed her the room and a chair.

At the door of this room, a policeman, in his flawlessly ironed uniform which was stiff like steel, wished to flaunt his authority, but was defeated and cogitated: 'I must remain detached, because though I salute you today, I may arrest you tomorrow.'

Govind is filling a sofa for two. Comfort and prosperity are flowing from his body like sweat. Two men are sitting on his two sides, a little behind him, and it looks like they are trying to prove their smartness at every moment. One of them is scribbling on a notebook continuously. The other is offering the phone receiver to the Minister after whispering to him, mouthpiece covered by his palm, and replacing it on the cradle after the conversation is over. The phone rings almost as soon as the receiver is replaced on the cradle. A hard bound notebook is lying on the sofa table. (Kunti remembered that many days ago she had asked a girl in her class to go out because the girl had not brought a hard bound notebook. The impecunious father of the girl was outraged and withdrew the girl from the school putting an end to her education.) People are sitting very close to each other on long benches along the wall, so close they cannot move their faces to left or right. There are people everywhere: the lawn that was, veranda, every room in the house, kitchen, toilets, gods' room; everywhere that humid stale sweaty odour, gibber and jabber, betel chewer's spit, smoke of tobacco rolled in tendu leaves, gossips of irony, bitching and boasting.

Kunti thought that she will run to Govind, though his face is now rotund like ripe *guamala* pumpkin, an exotic breed of pumpkin of her area. His head is half bald, he is wearing weird eyeglasses, and his belly has bulged out and lay on his lap. Yet why do he and his face appear so much as your own? What is there in human face that even with long lapse of time, long experience of cruelty, conflict and separation, indifference and selfishness the face looks so familiar, so comforting and reassuring?

Govind listened to each visitor like a competent political administrator, took decision on each case, and did not see Kunti arriving or her excitement. After a long time, when Kunti was overtaken by dreams of many incidents which were reduced to zero now and which did not happen anyway, when her mind had wandered away, her turn came. The minister gave her as much time as he gave to each visitor. Kunti told her name and the name of her village. The minister increased the width of his smile a tiny bit and said to his support staff: 'That is where my sharecropper revolution started.' And he asked Kunti to sit down. But he did not embrace her, he did not kiss her, he did not address her as *my queen*, there was no shower of flowers from heaven on the great moment of their meeting, and wild birds did not sing in unison.

Kunti became depressed and melancholic, she cried inside in utter helplessness and wailed silently: 'Papa, ma, I had to be subjected to this humiliation too.' She tried to remember them, but she could not even recall her father's face. Govind was laughing like laughing Buddha, the wire of his artificial tooth showed, and he looked at the virgin breasts of Kunti. *Kunti is seeing that she and Govind are very small children roaming in the village forest, they are gathering coloured stones, the end of her little sari tears with the weight of the stones. At home, her mother slaps her for ruining her sari. They were catching damselflies near the brook. Govind was not good in studies, when the teacher raised the cane, his sinless pink lips quivered as if the wind is kissing him. And when Kunti looks at him, both angry and tearful, Govind forgets the pain of the striking cane and smiles just to console her. How his heart was transparent and liquescent like hail!*

On hearing about her transfer, when Govind nodded his head in sympathy, the reflection from his eyeglasses jumped over the carpet which had been beautiful in the past and hopped like two ugly moths on the wall. The impatient urgency and ridicule for Kunti of other petitioners is pushing her out, and the judicious indifference of Govind is making her helpless. He asked, as she was going out: 'How have you come, have you eaten anything?'

This is also a game, Kunti realized. Yet, she was grateful. As she went out of the room, with a strange and inexplicable sense of glory, her feet did not touch the ground. She recalled a scene from her childhood. *While roaming in the forest barefoot, a thorn pierced her foot and Govind removed this thorn with the help of a stronger thorn of another tree, and then Kunti hugged him tightly to escape the pain. But in course of time, the memory of the scene mutated to one where Govind was kissing her foot.*

Outside the room, most of the people were talking in whispers and signs, and most of them had come to either get transferred or get a transfer cancelled of the visitor or someone else. Govind sent someone to Kunti to get her dropped at the bus terminal, but the driver was not found, he had gone to drop someone else. A sweeper in dirty clothes and an out of shape eyeglasses told a fat and prosperous looking man in a spotless safari suit: 'Sir, your shirt has a black patch.'

As she returned by bus to her place and her house, their greater proximity burnt her with a massive sense of humiliation. The bus stopped near the banyan tree as this was the bus stop for the area, and a squirrel was scampering about under the tree waiting for a mina, little cormorant or some other bird to drop off a seed after eating the fruit. Kunti chastened the squirrel silently: 'Your forefathers had built the Rama Setu for god Rama to cross the sea and reach Sri Lanka, and here you are waiting for a left-over of some bird?'

Two days after Kunti met Govind, when he had gone to the toilet to pee, (he did not have proper urination because of some problem in either the kidney or the urinary bladder or both, two specialist doctors were treating him, could not agree on the line of treatment, and before they could converge to a course of treatment), and Govind had left the discussion with a businessman halfway, and was drawing up a strategy on how the bribe money can be raised so that his share will go up keeping the share of the political party intact, Dami's father appeared before him and asked: 'You did not care to look up my children, you did not help them when they are in the dumps, when they are almost starving! Or have you decided to go to hell with the loads of sin on your shoulders?'

Govind, thoroughly frightened, glanced at the toilet door and found it bolted from inside. He blabbered in desperate hurry: 'Yes, yes, I will look them up, I will take care of them, besides I did not know that you will die, I had only raised my hand to frighten you.' At this moment a piece of square tile was dislodged from the ceiling, fell on the bald scalp of Govind and disappeared into the toilet. Twenty-four hours later, in the largest hospital of the country, the brain and heart of Govind became dead.

Seven days later, Kunti resigned from her job and arranged to return to her ancestral village. Of course, it took several days for her to reach her village.

THREE

By the time Kunti grew to childhood, India had not become free from British occupation. But most Indians believed that India will become free and very soon. Though Kunti's father did not quite believe that India will become free, he had hung outside on the wall of each side of the only door of the puja room, the gods' sanctorum, a photo each of Gandhi and Gopabandhu. Gandhi was famous as a leader of freedom movement. Gopabandhu, senior to Gandhi, was a down-to-earth social reformer and educationist of Odisha province and was known for his work for the needy including of rescue and relief during natural calamities like flood. Kunti's father could not see anything to gain or lose in the country becoming independent or continuing with the occupation. He was not a landlord with administrative powers that he would lose villages under him to the government, nor he would have lost land under his personal cultivation. On the contrary, his personal land was duly settled in his name, he paid the land rent regularly and he kept the land papers in order. Irrespective of who was in charge of looking after the country, his financial condition could not have gone in only one direction, either only prosperity or only destitution.

Those days a Brahmin conversant with principles of law and justice and with a longish and thin pigtail on the backside of head, and more often other persons who were considered gentlemen often for obscure reasons, interfered in the affairs of simple farmers and caused a commotion usually with no personal motives for gain. These mediators were called the five wise men or *panchayat*.

Those days a religious mendicant with a long pigtail, after begging for uncooked rice for seven days, (No, he did not really beg, he sang classic religious songs composed with special metres, and excerpts from Puranas, in baritone voice.) and since the rice he had brought was not enough, he took his seven children to the forest and sold them off to tiger uncle for two large meals. When the monk returned with two meals a mischievous imp took away the meals.

Let us take another example. A man became insane which made him hate everything or made him incurably ill, because of evil witchcraft by his brother's wife, or because the ghost of an old man who died on a Friday lost its way (such a ghost was called *pushkar*) and possessed the man by riding over his neck. The man left his village. His brothers called the five wise men of the village and made a plan for the management of the share of the property of their insane brother. The country became independent, the insane brother recovered from his illness and returned. He asked for his share in the property. He filed litigations in the courts. These cases were continuing in the courts even when Kunti finished her studies and left the village to take up the job of a school teacher. The old people of the village let out long sighs and lamented: 'Aha, how quickly such disputes were resolved during British occupation! When our elders adjudicated over disputes, they always looked at the moral aspect of it. Where is that moral aspect now?'

(Here, they will give five or six examples of their

dispensation of justice.) Of course, it was never said by anyone that each of the old gentlemen had a couple of cases in government courts. But who has ever heard that someone has land, but does not have a single litigation in any government court?

Though there were in force social mores and traditions set up in independent India and formal laws made by the colonial government, there was a subtle distinction in its application to people according to their position in society. When Dasia, hailing from a poor community, was going to marry a child-widow (whose marriage had not been consummated), did not the elders hold a meeting and stop the marriage? And did not the elders seize a pair of bullocks belonging to Dasia and auction it, so that Dasia does not repeat such mistakes in future. The money was kept under the safe custody of Panchu Pradhan, who was a solvent and reliable gentleman of the village and, of course, he wrote a receipt for this. This money has not been recovered from Panchu Pradhan for a village function yet; but during the British rule, would the money have been left unrecovered? Again, when the child-widow, who had become an adult, took shelter in the house of Panchu Pradhan, and when she became pregnant entirely of her own fault, should the elders have awarded the same punishment to Panchu Pradhan? What is just and fair for a gentleman cannot be made applicable to Dasia, a man from a poor community.

When the future was foretold, it was not accepted word for word, an analysis was made, several interpretations evolved, and then the forecast was understood correctly. When Kunti was born and the village astrologer drew up her horoscope and among some inscrutable verbiage (for example: the holder of the horoscope will usher in good times for her parents, she will face danger not from fire, not from water, she will face danger from wind) predicted that if she gets married, she will be a queen, and if she does not get married, she will become a fairy, the parents concluded that she will become a queen. Whoever could even think in those days that a girl would not marry? It was possible for a girl to commit suicide, but it was impossible to think that a girl would not marry.

Kunti's village Ankamara was ancient and hoary like Veda, Hindu Purana and folktales. At one end of the village resided a sanyasi of Alekh sect, which believed in one Brahmam, and meditation and singing paeans for Him as the sole path to be merged with Him. The landlord and some villagers had built a little thatched ashram for him and had donated some land. (The villagers were not anxious to donate land to the sanyasi, but they came to realize that all unforeseeable dangers to the village were coming from this unprotected direction.) Every evening three to four persons gathered on the veranda of the ashram, sang paeans, played tambourines and smoked a little hashish. The egregious calamities and various forms of evil spirits which rolled down from the hills behind the ashram were stopped and made to go back by the sanyasi.

On another side, the Goddess of Forests resided on the hill. Her decor was graceful, elegant and melodious. On the side of the river, the Goddess of Path was worshipped under a banyan tree. That side was full of slippery and soft slush and mud. The sides of the village which were covered by hills were formidable with thick forests and wild animals.

People from other villages said with less mirth and more malice that Ankamara is so inaccessible that the

Goddess of Cholera and Other Epidemics does not enter the village. This was a syrupy aphorism because despite all these obstacles, the Goddess of Cholera and Other Epidemics entered Ankamara and took away Kunti's father.

Later in the autumn of the year when the pole-juggler at the annual worship of Goddess Durga was possessed by the Goddess, and the juggler whirled horizontally on the pole, he revealed that on the night before the worship of Goddess of Cholera and Other Epidemics, a pedestrian had peed near the abode of the goddess. Therefore the Goddess of Forests could not protect the village from the Goddess of Cholera and Other Epidemics. (It is said that the pedestrian was later afflicted with leprosy, but this gave no consolation to the family members of Kunti.) That is why though the Goddess of Forests had looked cheerful and picturesque, she had actually been polluted and debilitated. The Goddess of Forests was consecrated a second time; but Kunti's father did not come back.

Kunti was a student when her father died. She had a younger brother called Gobara who was small, and so small that some people called him a mouse. She also had three elder brothers and one elder sister. Girls from houses, where there was sufficient food, used to learn a few things in the village elementary school. The obloquy that education of girls led to loss of honour came to be in vogue years later. If a girl could study up to class Three, she was considered educated and a symbol of women's education. Kunti decided, all by herself, to study further so that she will become great and venerable. She studied with earnestness though she was not very intelligent. But some children, like Govind, who were more intelligent than her, slipped away from the elementary school and plucked blue berries from thorny hedges or with sling shots felled the nests of innocent little eagles whose nests were perched on big mango trees.

Even Sarang who had been Kunti's classmate dropped out from school and was engaged as a regular farm-hand in her house on yearly basis.

In fourth and fifth classes, Kunti was the only regular girl student. It was arduous to learn a completely new language like English, and a strangely articulated Mathematics; but the teachers showed enormous patience in teaching her. In such environment, some malicious gossip and calumny was bound to come up. In fact a rumour spread out rapidly that a dark-skinned teacher was going to marry her. But long before Kunti reached the age to marry, the teacher studied as a non-collegiate student, took the degree examination, acquired BA degree, took the competitive examination for Subordinate Civil Service, was selected as a Sub-Deputy Collector and joined the State government as a Land Officer and Junior Magistrate.

Kunti had heard of some fragments of the rumour about her marriage, and when the teacher went away, nothing happened to her except a brief throb in her chest. Thereafter she did not know whether she remembered the teacher or had completely forgotten him.

Some years later, when Bhanu was not coming to her anymore, once Kunti dreamt that she was cleaning with soap a bucketful of dirty briefs of that dark-skinned teacher, and when she went to the water tap to wash them, even a drop of water did not come out of the tap.

Before Govind left the high school, Kunti was walking with him for about a mile to reach the high school from her village on every school day. During rainy season when paddy stalks grew tall or when flood waters filled the pedestrian path through paddy fields, they took a different road which did not get submerged, but was two miles longer. Kunti had a different visage and she carried herself with a certain elegance. When most of the students wore homemade palm-leaf hats in rainy season, Kunti went to school holding a colourful umbrella. (Her father had bought this from a pilgrimage many years ago.)

Govind and Kunti exchanged books and handwritten notes in the school. They were quite efficient in this. Of course, in such transactions they did not need to use their own intelligence. The novels in the personal boxes of daughters-in-law of their clan, who were the clan sisters-in-law of Kunti, provided enough information about the practices and the contents of letters exchanged between a boy and a girl. Besides, the village library had a stock of such novels which Govind accessed, though they were less exciting than those fished out of the boxes of clan sisters-in-law. The "love letters" Kunti wrote to Govind had adages and gnomes, riddles and ditties, a stanza from a metrical folk song with four stanzas and other traditional lyrical poems. And she addressed Govind as *my king, my Krishna, the jewel of my eyes* and similar terms of endearment.. Kunti found the name Govind so commonplace and trite that she could not find a real lovable address or write a real love letter. At the end of the letter, she signed as *your unfortunate destitute, your undeserving lover for life, the humble slave of your lotus feet, the humble mate in all your future births* etc.

Govind came to Ankamara whenever he could find an alibi, and to find an alibi he even made a friendship with Nathu Mahalik, who was a snotty dumb nincompoop.

Govind had to cross a river to come to Ankamara village. In summer the stones and sand in the river became very hot. In the rains, the poles of the boat did not reach the ground. People from other villages joked that the villagers of Ankamara performed their morning ablutions in boats.

Govind left the school, withdrew from formal education and when asked by anyone said that he will join the independence movement and become an armed revolutionary. But by then the country had become free from British occupation, and there was no Hindu Muslim riot in this part of the country. Therefore, he joined the sharecropper movement. This was more fun for him because he could stand on the land of another person who had the full right, title and possession of the land, he could challenge the legal owner loudly and aggressively, and ten persons hovered around him with borrowed courage. Soon a situation came when he could not meet Kunti much, and eventually they could not meet at all. However, the rumour about his clandestine affair with Kunti resurfaced from time to time. When he was asked whether the alleged affair was true, Govind did not say a word, smiled an enigmatic smile and reinforced everyone's suspicion.

Many years later, when Kunti was returning to her village Ankamara, and saw that the crossing on the main road from where a road had branched to her village now had a signboard which read "Road to Ankamara Irrigation Project", she did not remember Govind, she did not remember when the first proposal for her marriage came to their home, just as she could not remember when she had seen for the first time her mother's face or the village goddess.

But she remembered the first time she had noticed

the sweets maker. He made the sweets at home and sold it to households. He also made larger quantity of sweets during festive seasons and set up shop at fairs and operas. He belonged to a caste which made sweets and also cooked in large feasts like in weddings. The family kept to itself the culinary skill and passed it only to the next generation. That day the sweets maker had brought some fried things soaked in sugar syrup. Kunti remembered that he always had a quarter of a smile hanging from his face, as if he was a kid and was just going to get a piece of sweet. Kunti's mother gave a seer of rice, about one and half kilogram, to him and bought some sweets, gave to her and said in a low voice: 'Take this and eat it alone silently in some corner. Otherwise, the whole clan will start a ruckus. The sweets maker has come like Saturn, the planet-god which will cause discord.'

Later when Kunti ran the astrological period of Saturn-god, she suffered from hemorrhoids, her body gained weight around her torso, her face became odd shaped as if it had been sketched by a small child, and the Secretary of the school management committee single-handedly disgraced her in that small scandal-mongering town, her colleague Kunja challenged her to her face, 'Why have you trapped that kid Bhanu, may I hear?' Her days stretched out to horrendous nightmarish lengths like it happens in the mirrors of a magic house and the nights swelled up to terrorizing darkness. Then Kunti did not understand why and how the sweets maker with a quarter of smile, whose only resemblance was with god Krishna of wall calendars, is creating such an enormous amount of pain and disarray for her.

That day Kunti's eyes became moist with her mother's

affection; but she could not eat the sweets alone at the corner of their granary made of mature and seasoned wood. She hid the sweets in a joint between two pieces of wood and looked for elder brother Balia. The foolish boy that he was, Balia was reading a book in the near-darkness of twilight and he took quite long to understand why he was being summoned. They came to the joint, but the sweets were not there, nor anyone could find out who had eaten the sweets, whether any person, mouse, cat or goddess Thorn-eater, not even until Balia died of gastro-intestinal disease at the age of eight. 'You cheated me,' Balia howled loudly. His elder brother learnt of their mother's clandestine sale of one and half kg of rice. He called his mother "forsaken by goddess Lakshmi". Throughout the night, the brother and his wife fought, and a few days later he and his wife and children separated from rest of the family with their share of land on this pretext.

Before the separation of the eldest son, his wife and children from the rest of the family, the five village gentlemen were called for a fair partition. Kunti's family was among the well off and respected families of the village and in such cases the mediation is often not effective. But all the knotty issues were discussed, the marriage of Kunti was discussed, and Kunti remembered for a long time that it was decided that Kunti will marry before Balia, and half of the marriage expenses will be borne by the eldest two brothers and the rest will be the responsibility of other family members.

Whenever a proposal for the marriage of Kunti came, her mother jumped like a simpleton and she ran to the two goddesses protecting the triangular village and made vows. On every such occasion she asked the village priest to invoke the goddess who possessed one of the regular devotees who answered mother's questions, and with two goddesses such invocation happened twice a month. She will spread a layer of questions on the possessed devotees and even the Alekh sanyasi, and onlookers will chortle behind her. All of them will give datelines by tenth day of Phalguna month in autumn, twenty-seventh day of Phalguna, fifth day of Baishakh in summer, twelfth day of Ashadh in rainy season. The possessed ones gave away a lot of picturesque and unnecessary description: the groom will be from north, south-west, south, or north-east; he would be rich, well modestly rich; very fair, somewhat darkish complexion; of average height, moderately built; there is a place of worship near the house; the house is made of lime mortar; there will be a Chinese Honeysuckle creeper with red flowers at the entrance; on the north-east side there will be a small pond; the elder brother of the groom will be working overseas in armed forces.

Mother returned from the puja and built houses of various shapes and colours in her mind's sky, and managed to remain happy for some days. When they received new clothes as part of several rites from clan people and her parents, she saved them so that they will be useful in Kunti's wedding. She was worked up when her late husband's brother removed clay from the front of the house; if the place is dug out, how can a wedding platform be constructed there?

The summer leaves with Baishakh and Jyestha months. The foretold date for wedding moves surprisingly to rainy months Ashadh and Shravan though most almanacs do not have dates for wedding in rainy season. There are no auspicious dates for some months, and the astrologer gives fresh dates for the autumn month of Margashira.

The daughter of eldest brother of Kunti attained marriageable age; that was when Kunti had to appear the important Board examination for matriculation. Her brother went to a tantric with the astrologer. From the esoteric discourse of the tantric, the astrologer's sphere of knowledge expanded, there were many obstacles for the wedding, both Mars and Jupiter are causing inauspicious influence, but the hard and unfortunate circumstances were not insurmountable with some help from gods and planets, because the moon has auspicious influence on the seventh house of the horoscope of the girl. Rites of *shantikarana* (prayer for pacification of planets who had inauspicious influence) and *uchhatana* (elevating the good influence of mildly favourable planets) were performed according to tantric procedure. While Kunti recited "Om imamdeva..asa..." mantra facing the north-west direction for pacification of moon god, she passed matriculation. On one Thursday she wrote down "the great planet Jupiter mantra" on a paper, covered it in plastic and cloth and tied it on her left arm with thread she had rolled from cotton with her palms. With the help of her extended relations in the area, she joined as a teacher in a just opened high school sixty kilometres away and taught others on subjects she had not understood well, and received shelter like a girl's blouse swaying alone on a clothesline under torrential rains. What kind of shelter is this, which lets loose the most important part of life alone and helpless and the rest parts of life are rolled into some bundle and shoved into a corner behind a heavy piece of sawn wood?

She was not divinely beautiful, but she was not ugly either. Again, there was no girl in the area who did not find anyone to marry because she was ugly. Her brothers were not reckless in charity to sell off their property for the wedding expenses, but they would have paid enough for a decent and appropriate wedding. Except for some tittle-tattle, she had no ineligibility for marriage and which young girl did not have some tittle-tattle around her? Nevertheless, that auspicious moment slipped out of her closed palm and she did not know why. A few days after she took up the job, she took from her three brothers and a sister their obsessive righteousness and took her mother to her house near the school where she taught.

For her mother, this house was very different. Loneliness swept in from outside world right into the house. Mother said: 'My daughter, are you looking around? Can you see anyone? Have you kept this before your eyes? Are you saving some money or not? Even if someone has lost his first wife, why not consider him? You are losing the shine of your face and body. If you look so pale, who will look at you?'

Kunti heard her mother's gabble and blather every day and was worried that she was growing old and losing the efficiency of her sensory organs, and as they said in the village she has begun to burn away. But mother had really become night-blinded because she had been unable to see the scene of wedding of Kunti even after such an endless protraction, and decided that there was no other scene worth watching in her life.

Kunti became furious inside her and thought: 'Did you look for a husband yourself? Shall I look for my husband all by myself?'

But Kunti said briefly: 'I am fine, the way I am.'

Many days after this dialogue between Kunti and her mother, when she had resigned from her job and decided to go to her village and saw the signboard "Road to Ankamara Irrigation Project" and remembered the son (who was said to resemble the strict Saturn planet-god) of the sweets maker, she did not remember Govind at all. She did not remember any juicy scandal. For a moment she thought that many people in the village will remember her and hug her and carry her into the village, a sudden doubt sprang up that no one will recognize her, and she put a halt to her hopes. She also did not remember when she had heard the unnecessary, unrealistic and irrelevant news that their country had become independent – as if it was not their country which was becoming independent; another country in another continent had become independent. But she thought that in the evening she will enjoy the *khanjani* which was a jangling little drum and tambourine with devotional songs. Thereafter, she became so immersed in the songs and music that she did not remember Govind.

She alighted from the bus at the crossing where the signboard was and a road branched off to her village from the main road. There were a couple of cabins made from coal tar coated wood planks on the roadside at the crossing and one of the cabins was a salon for hair cutting. She smiled when she read the signboard: they always make mistakes like this in government, they have converted "village" to "irrigation project". The priest in a clean long *fatei* and a brownish dhoti turned towards her when he saw her smile and knitted his brow. At that age, Kunti made many plans which were useful for the society and the country; but were completely irrelevant and useless for her. Rectification of such aberrations in signboards with the use of horse-whip was included among her plans. Her other plans included control of street violence by organized gangs which was a new trend in the area, stop theft of subsidized essential food items by black-marketers and their sale at higher rates, and shoot down education inspectors who took money for preparation of salary bills and for transfers. She has mellowed down with age and does not get as outraged now as she was in the younger days.

Kunti called a cycle-rickshaw and told him to take her to Ankamara. The rickshaw guy behaved as if he could not understand and Kunti suspected that he wanted to bargain for more fare. Kunti thought: 'He does not know that I am from this village, even if I have returned after a long time. But does this mean he will cheat me?'

She asked the rickshaw guy his name, his father's name, name of his village and then told him her father's name; but he remained silent and did not utter a word nor could recognize her.

She sat on the rickshaw and she was transposed to a world of colour like the lesson books of primary school: in winter mornings, the dewed village street, stacks of paddy straw in the barn, early morning threshing of paddy stalks under the hoofs of bullocks, the motley jabbering of people wrapped in blankets waiting to go to the paddy fields, a crowd sitting around a hearth on which large pots of water and raw paddy is boiled for making par-boiled paddy. From par-boiled paddy, par-boiled rice will be made which stays longer and is healthier food. The sun is playing truant and not coming out. The road near the house of Nathu Mahalik is slushy and grandmother's unruly black cow whose milk is sweet is tethered there.

In the evening of one full moon day, in front of the abode of the Goddess of Forests, lighted jute sticks are offered to the sky to invoke the souls of ancestors, the souls come in darkness but return

happily in the lighted path to heaven. The flames from jute sticks
rise high and in the eyes of a little Kunti they reach the moon.

On the day the Village Goddess comes out of her abode at
the roots of a banyan tree, a small area is dug out. Wood shavings,
twigs and leaves burn and fragrant myrrh and herbs are put on
this. This is lighted with burning charcoal. Water is sprinkled on
this bed when flames come out or the bed is too hot. When she had
walked on the fire, the fire was quite warm, at some spots hot and
singed slightly, but mostly it tingled the feet and did not hurt.
The man or woman who was possessed ate tiny clay horses.

The rickshaw stopped with a jerk. There is a
tall embankment in the front. On the other side of the
embankment, water reaches up to the hills. The rest of the
river cannot be seen. Kunti's village has been obliterated
with its mammoth heritage and innumerable sagas and
legends. Only then she remembered that she had known
from the day it happened that Ankamara village had been
submerged under the dam, and she had forgotten it.

There is a gentle breeze, and waves with slender
waists swam on the water.

The hill which had been so green has become bare and
rocky. No other trace of the village remained except the barren
cliffs, though she could not understand how she can say that
these barren cliffs had belonged to Ankamara village.

Kunti remembered a tale of a prince and a fairy that she
had heard from her grandma long ago. The fairy was crying on
the ghat of a beautiful pond of crystal-transparent water and the
ghat was made of spotlessly white marble. She was crying because
she had been cursed. At the end of the story, the fairy was released
from the curse because of the gallantry and valour of the prince.
As she returned to her celestial abode, she assured the prince: 'We

will be united in the next birth.' (The next part was quite another tale.) But no one agreed with this tragic end and grandma had to get the prince and fairy married at the end of the story.

Kunti knew that if she wished hard enough, she can become a water-fairy and search for and salvage her past, the blueberry shrub forest submerged in the dam, her necklace of red-and-black *gunja* seeds, and the prince of the fairy tale who was roaming in the river in her dreams. She will find the world she had seen through spectacles having blue plastic pieces for the eyepieces, her younger brother Gobara whose naked body looked like a rabbit, the canopied *ber* berries tree near the school. In the open air opera, war, martial musical instruments and just when the prince was going to be murdered by the villain, he is saved by the bright and intelligent princess. In the Calcutta-returned hands of father, bags full of printed frocks and a pair of trousers for eldest brother. In the campus of ashram of Alekh baba, fragrance of pomelo and lemon and the colour of red hibiscus flowers. She will snatch away mornings of fulgent dew drops, mornings of pearl drops from the hands of time. The low feeling of adolescent spring, some coyness puts you to silence, the breeze of spring rips away all uncertainty. An unfelt solitude freezes inside and makes you desolate, shorn off everything. You know you have lost something, but you cannot understand what it was, like an emptiness descends when a girl from a nearby village marries and goes away.

Kunti did not gather anything. She did not want to carry anything with her. She was crushed and spiritless. She was surprised that a few years ago something which would have made her whirl in a hurricane did not touch her now.

'What remains after all relationships cease to exist?' she asked herself, but did not know with which kind of wisdom or in which language she could answer this.

When she descended from the dam with quick steps, she knew that if she wished she could fly away like a fairy, but desisted from any such adventure. She descended slowly with firm and measured footsteps and sat on the rickshaw.

On the way back, the rickshaw guy said: 'The top of temple that you can see inside the dam was the temple of Alekh sanyasi. Everyday he walks on the water to reach his temple. Every night he sings melancholic prayers while playing *khanjani*, the little jingle drum. His prayers rend the heart. No one knows when he comes back. People have only seen him walking on water going to the temple.'

A few days later Kunti went to the settlement where displaced people of Ankamara had been shifted.

FOUR

At first a man in a tunic that had a circular and shining insignia made of brass and another contractor with the frame of a hippo reached the settlement and measured a piece of land from among grotesque boulders, clumsy stones and red pebbles. The sun shone brightly then and a white dusty smoke was coiling skywards. The gravitas they wore and their air of emanating omniscience helped to make a stray guess that they were from the government. They put up an illegible notice scribbled on a clay-coloured paper at one end of the settlement, and collected thumb impressions of some naked, illiterate children. The news spread from ear to ear that the owner of the land was returning; but there were two opinions on who the owner was. One, he is stinking rich, and is returning with a hidden treasure. Two, he is returning as a pauper, social outcast, with no other option and hopeless.

Most of the people wished that the one returning be rich; but the erstwhile landlord Ramachandra Mangaraj, who, atoning for the sins committed by his ancestors was now starving about fifteen days in a month, pooh-poohed the version: 'Let go, abandon your hopes. He must be a beggar from somewhere.' (In fact, the real name of the landlord was not Ramachandra Mangaraj. He had enacted in this character's role as a child artist in the village opera and had thus acquired this name.)

The time Kunti reached the village, cobwebs of darkness had spread everywhere; so, when she entered her new house many had not noticed her. But people in any case had little faith in witnesses and firsthand knowledge. Chakrapani said: 'The palanquin she was travelling in had brass lion cubs as legs, and the cubs looked wilted and despondent; as though the little doe they had caught as their prey had escaped into the darkness outside.'

'The lion cubs were of gold,' asserted Jatadhari.

'She came flying in the palanquin,' said Sakei, the sobbing one and Jatadhari's wife.

Kunti looked lustreless, of course, like a withered drumstick that had dried up from the tips; but from her looks the debate remained unsettled whether she had returned as a childless widow or a spinster who had crossed marriageable age. She was clad in a white sari with a border, but the border was so thin that it was not clear if it was a dhoti meant for a widow or a sari.

'A dhoti,' said Makara's mother.

'A sari,' said Sania's mother.

'Lo, Kunti, why have you shrunk and thinned down dear?' said Nephidi's mother. 'We have been through childbirths and diseases and go on in one piece; you have lived a comfortable life and yet you have become like a moth-eaten twig?'

Kunti refused to acknowledge that she knew anyone. She silently rejected the varied attempts and skills by men and women of myriad age groups who came to infiltrate into her life. She ignored silently the people who thronged around her, the villagers, her clan relations and other kith and kin. She was indifferent to discussions on the alleged disputes about her house, backyard, front yard, farm land and common land of the village, the volunteering touts and the elders who settled village issues and litigations. She declined silently to participate in the *homa* or fire offerings before Gods and Goddesses and with the entranced *kalisi* through whom the deities foretold the future, and prescribed solutions for the problems of the village. She refused the southerly spring wind, the lapwings, the catapults and tongue-twisters like *rama's mother-mother's sister rama's groom*. She did not participate in discussions on dowries and gifts, festivities and the village club, and the wedding rite of consecration of the bride and the groom with turmeric paste and fragrant flowers.

The village Goddess possessed Jatadhari. People nowadays ridiculed in the open his divination power. The priestess had carried along the Goddess of the old village to the new settlement at the time of shifting, though the village Goddess had not been consecrated at the new site. Only when dynamites were detonated in the mines at the foothills and the new settlement quaked with the impact, the settlers recalled that the village Goddess had not been consecrated. Around the full-moon night of Pousha, the coldest month of the lunar calendar, people who had already been feeling hopeless like trees washed clean of earth at the roots, suddenly felt a bit sheltered. They consecrated the Goddess within three days hoping that all hopelessness would end with the presence of the living Goddess. The Brahmin priest from another village who came to enthrone the goddess and perform the rites had come riding a bicycle and the people sighed: 'Ah, what eon of Kaliyuga nowadays, what eon of unjustness and irreligiousness! The priest is riding a bicycle. And this guy's son is riding a motorbike in the town on his rounds to perform sacred rites!'

When the Goddess possessed Jatadhari, he oracled: 'The miracles and powers of the Goddess will manifest in Kunti someday or the other.'

Kunti (who did not experience menopause though she had crossed the age for it) heard this announcement; but did not say anything.

Days after this, Kunti had once gone to see the throne of the Goddess. The Goddess had been enshrined in an alcove constructed of neatly arranged boulders. Because, in that craggy settlement there was not even a bush of creeper grass growth, forget a banyan, under whose shadow, She could have been enthroned. White cliffs rose behind the abode of the Goddess. Though the settlement had come up only recently, the people talked with great conviction that due to some curse some white-skinned foreigners had turned into the white rocks there.

Before long, every possible piece of gossip that could have been concocted about Kunti was created and eventually exhausted. A few fatherly men had kept in their memories undamaged stories of Kunti's education, and Govind's participation in the share-cropper movement. One old uncle had even remembered the dark-complexioned male teacher (with whom Kunti had shared a childhood scandal), though in his hazy, wily memory, through time, the dark-complexioned teacher had become fair-complexioned. Many of these old persons were not free from the petty feuds of that time and the consequent civil and criminal lawsuits. The old folks did not command respect anymore; because after the old village was submerged and the people left their ancestral homesteads, all the predictions of the old folks were proved to be wrong and all their pragmatic knowledge of the world was found to be useless. The young blockheads always carried an arrogant belief that the old people had absolutely no role in the setting up of the new settlement.

These apart, the old people with their demeanours provided perfect material for mirth. Which onlooker could escape from laughing over these idiosyncrasies? Let's say, in someone's house, at the place meant for the kitchen in the old village, now stood a wall in the new settlement. They had been living for some time in the new settlement, yet had not been used to the alteration; they hit their heads on the wall, where there should have been the door to the kitchen, like blind lambs and mud-plaster came off the termite-eaten walls. (Readers, please don't assume that I am alleging against the engineers who have built the houses in the new settlement. Firstly, I am narrating a tale, I must tell it straight, what business do I have to comment on others? Secondly, I am a poor innocent and insignificant chatterbox, what do I know about technical subjects?) And the place, where a niche had been carved in the wall of a particular house in the old village, was not fit for holding even a nail in the new settlement. First the people left their rooms and shifted to the verandas, and thereafter built wattle-and-daub huts in front of the houses and shifted there.

Moreover after all that Chandara, Markand's father did, could any young man or woman of the village retain his respect for these aging men and women? Years ago, during the second world war Chandara was wandering like he had a screw loose in his head and was apprehended for alleged espionage, and had been sent to jail for a few days. Shrewd Markand had manipulated the papers relating to the imprisonment of his father to ensure him a freedom fighter's pension, and was himself trying for a ticket from the ruling party to contest as a candidate for the head of the local self-government or panchayat. As per the law of the land then, the ownership and possession of the ancestral land and property went into the hands of the government and then it was acquired for the Ankamara irrigation project; but Markand's crazy father did not understand any law or regulation, he did not part with his land. Police arrested him under Section 109 of the Code of Criminal Procedure, for suspicious movements and his attempts to hide himself when accosted. When he returned after spending about a month in the prison, he went to the spot where his land had been, and knew that he could no more hold on to his land physically as the land had been submerged in the reservoir. The old man stopped talking and wandered around the dam. The police tried to threaten him, but he was not afraid, mad as he was. Needless to mention, no one else in the old village had gone to jail accused in a criminal case. Except for a man with elephantine legs – he was named Narada (his real name was something else, he had acted the role of Narada, the mythological Sage of the Heavens who carried and disseminated news among the three worlds of earth, heaven and the netherworld, as a child artist in the village opera, had quipped the sage's favourite overture "Narayan, Narayan!" and had thus acquired the name "Sage Narada"), he had been imprisoned for a month on the charge of theft of a pumpkin from someone's kitchen garden; after spending a month the counterfeit Narada had been released from the prison and had fled to Rangoon incognito. Yes, a government engineer of the irrigation project came to the settlement one day, bringing along Markand's father; but the sober, gentle, smart and aristocratic looking engineer sir was so voluminous that his body bumped against the verandas lining the houses on both sides of the lane, and neither straightways nor sideways could he enter into the village. He rebuked the villagers in English for their ignorance, superstitions, uncivilised habit of extending their houses to the road and went away; and lo, Chandara again returned to the dam. A week later his body was seen floating on the water; a magistrate's inquest report said that the death was due to an accident.

That Kunti knew black magic, and her glasses in real were an aid to cloud up others' vision – someone spread the message around and as a result, a brat or two of the village peered into her eyes through her glasses and got terrified. One of the boys caught fever which though was cured by malaria tablets, the sensational rumour that Kunti was a witch, generally held good, as it was more exciting. Chakrapani, the village tout and with a hairless scalp like a slab of black granite was trying to laugh off these rumours, but every time, the spittle of the betel cones he chewed sprayed on the listeners' faces.

(When the settlement was coming up and the court suites relating to acquisition of land was not settled yet, Chakrapani managed to enter in the government record-of-rights in his own name the four acres of land that had belonged to the four brothers of Makunda's household, and pocketed the compensation money paid for this land. One evening the four brothers caught hold of Chakrapani in a fit of wild rage, and pulled his hair so hard that half of it came out when he tried to escape; in a few days following this he lost the rest of his hair perhaps because of the dreadful memory of the incident, or otherwise, and became clean bald.)

One evening, after about a week of her coming to the settlement, Kunti lighted the evening wick near the holy basil plant, waited till the wick burnt away completely and the fire was snuffed out, and came inside her house. She closed the front door and turned back to peer at the courtyard. The courtyard was bright with a soft, tender and faint light; perhaps it was a moonlit night. Right there stood Chandara, Markand's father. On his scalp stood out as few swollen resolute veins as the few strands of hair there. His grin looked like a straw on a thatch darkened with time and rain. 'Lo grand uncle, when did you come?' asked Kunti.

The old man sat on the ground. After returning from the jail during the war he had made it into a habit not to sit on a smooth reed mat, or a coarse thick twine mat, or a cot, or a chair. Chandara had always been a blabbermouth. Sometimes he would say: 'O, that other tale apparently had been told to me by a wall of the jail and this story had been told to me by the *kadamba* tree in the jail compound.'

The garrulous habit had not left him after his death. He started: 'Dear daughter, your father had once saved me from committing an act that was a total violation of dharma. You know that I had a piece of land adjoining the village cremation ground (no, Kunti did not know this), you would not know how fertile or rich this little stretch of land was – you would not; did you ever look after cultivation of and harvest in village land? One day I was sizing the ridge between my land and the cremation ground, honestly, I had an evil design – to encroach into one fourth of an acre from the cremation ground and merge it to my land. Weeding operation was going on in the adjacent piece of land, six or seven persons were busy working there. Your father came and stood before me. He said: *What are you doing? Don't you*

see the pots and broken shards of clay pots still lying where I had
been burnt?

'Panicky, I sent for the surveyor and within five days measured the land and vacated the land of the burial ground to the last inch. But dear, I failed to understand your father's adjudication of justice and injustice. On the other side, Chakrapani has encroached so much of the cremation ground land, and why did your father not tell him a word?'

Old Chandara blabbered through the night, and Kunti, despite her indifference and detachment, acquired a good amount of general knowledge on the village. The village landlord – not the present one, the great great grandfather of the present landlord – was a terror. Once the old father of Chandrabhanu from the lower lane had walked past him with his shoes on and stamping, and had been fined one rupee. When the landlord strode on the village road, people knew that some calamity would befall the person whom he looked at squarely, and precisely for this reason a few families from the upper lane shifted to the lower lane and settled there in obscurity, away from the main street. He, during his salad days (he was not the landlord then), had been caught making love to a grown-up child-widow, was caught, thrashed, and had jumped into the neck-deep water of the river to commit suicide; he didn't die, he had bent his legs there covering his head with some lotus leaves. Towards the evening, he had fled to Burma; there he made handsome money from the business of sending human labour from Odisha to Burma, and returned to the village to buy the title and rights of the landlord.

But much later, during the peak of the share-croppers' movement, when an agitated mob broke into the landlord's house they saw a meagre man spread on a torn cloth mattress blowing up feeble nasalised coughs. The man got up from the bed and raised his eyes at the people; his eyeballs had sunk into their sockets. When the shocked and scared people backed away, Govind shouted: *Stop, don't go away.*

The frail, decrepit man in fact was the landlord. He looked up silently at the people, panting for breath; soon he lay down and coughed feebly as earlier, as if he was scared to do so loudly. The agitated crowd was abashed – as if a mountain that they were going to climb with gusto, excitement and challenges inexplicably vanished from their sight!

When Chandara went back after describing his anecdotes, Kunti had already fallen to sleep and did not know when he had left.

The next day, at the same evening hour, at the same place in the courtyard, Sundari's mother – Kunti's clan aunt – was standing. The courtyard was bathed in a deluge of moonlight, perhaps it was the waxing lunar phase; the wind was carrying down ferment and dust of heated stones, and the colloidal wind choked everyone. Kunti recollected that she had been very small, for some reason she does not remember anymore, the aunt overpowered her and tickled her so much that Kunti peed in her knickers. Now, after all these years, her body, inexplicably, feels ticklish the same way. Her body had the same titillation and cold creeps now after encountering Sundari's mother.

'No dear girl, I will not tickle you this time,' said Sundari's mother. 'Are you still the same little Kunti girlie today? No.'

'Aunt, I feel the same way even now,' Kunti said.

Aunt settled down there comfortably, without an invitation, hanging her legs down. 'Dear girl,' she started, 'do leave the paddy under the falling dew for a while in the night, if you rinse them in the moonlight, the paddy will yield rice grains having the colour and fragrance of white jasmine flowers. I could no longer pound paddy on the paddy-thresher as I grew older. Alo, my Sundari did not grow up like I had expected. She asked me once: Ma, be true, am I not prettier than Kunti, am I not fairer? Do I look ugly because of the tiny moles on the skin of my face? Then why does that dark-complexioned teacher peep only at Kunti's face? Alo, are you two not friends?

'Dear Ma, what is friendship without rivalry? If I don't envy her, how will my time pass?' She replied.

'What show-off is this dear? You know, Sundari's father did not possess even an inch of land, nor was he worth a pie when it comes to any worthwhile job! Six months in a year he slogged and drudged in the opera, and he was possessed by the addiction of opera, but the income from it did not meet his living and health expenses. Dear, is opera a joke? You and your troupe travel to faraway lands – Tata, Rangoon, Tekali. They do not sleep for nights and days. Yet, knowing all this I had my own aches that he would not find food for us. I understand everything, but what could I do? I had always thought, Govinda will marry Sundari; but he did not.

'One day, while I was pounding paddy, Sundari fell from my womb. Her head would have been crushed, but for an inch. Even our homestead land was dragged into a court litigation, which took twenty-one years six months and two days to end. Before the litigation ended, knowing that we would not win the case, my forbearance held no longer, I quietly drew my last breath, and died.'

After his wife passed away Sundari's father left the opera and worked as a serf for the lawyer to pay for the expenses of his court cases. When the dam project ensued, many outsiders came. They earned a lot. Sundari had been staying alone. During this time Sundari became the first ever prostitute in the thousand-year-old history of Ankamara village. When the village was submerged, the civil suits on Sundari's homestead land had been settled; but the criminal cases were still continuing, and so Sundari could not get a plot in the new settlement. She disappeared. Kunti remembered, years ago, when Govind had just given up studies, and was taken for a truant and a loafer by everyone, and he had come to Kunti's house in the early hours of the evening. Ah, how the jasmines bloomed in loads spread over the jasmine-wing of the school garden! As if the blooms had anticipated his arrival! Sundari came over to borrow some curd. Kunti's elder sister-in-law (who was pretty as a fairy in children's story books when she had just been married, and now, through with hassles of separation of land among her husband's brothers, four childbirths, anger and the arrogance and vanity spawned from possession of twenty-eight quintals of paddy in the granary per year, behaved like a dried leaf catching fire) grumbled. Kunti intervened and got the curd from the kitchen saying that she would have the curd herself, and gave it to Sundari. Sundari took the curd and gave it to Govind, but did not reveal that she had got it from Kunti. Everyone in Kunti's family, however, came to know of this, later in the night. Kunti had to answer a whole bunch of straight and crooked jibes. Govind's intelligence being like the eye of a fly – mixed-up, complex and imperfect, he did not understand anything.

Those were the days when reading hygiene in the

school syllabus made you hate the water of the village pond. When Kunti drank the water from a pond she felt as if bacteria were wriggling in her mouth, down through the throat pipe and to the stomach. Those were the days when you could boast about the moles on the covered parts of your body; when tender, new born human voices could bloom like blossoms. Yet Sundari, in the thousand-year-old ancestry of Ankamara had to become the first ever prostitute.

'My dear sweet aunt,' Kunti said choking with emotion, 'the poor girl had to suffer so much! Had I known, I would have taken her with me.'

'I know dear girl,' said aunt, 'where ever Sundari might be, she would come back if she is alive. She would come back too, I know, even if she is dead.'

FIVE

Every kind of person from her village and from other villages came to Kunti with all kinds of problems. People with headaches, rheum and bile problems. Parents of a two year old child suffering from incurable chronic ailments. Educated as well as illiterate people losing and winning in court litigations. People inflicted with lunatic ghosts, blood sucking devils and adrift witches who had lost their way. People who had lost cows, calves and gold. People in search of jobs. People in search of suitable husbands for the unwed girls in their houses. People who came with complaints against the school teacher who skipped school almost every day and was busy with petty public matters which did not concern him. People who came with grievances about the government shop which did not get subsidized stocks of rice and sugar in time for sale.

Kunti was not anxious to solve any of the problems. (She was never famous as a social worker or activist.) Sometimes she uttered a word or a phrase, and the listeners made some sense or other out of it. Sometimes she smiled gently and said: 'I am just an old woman, what can I know?' She did not smile only; with a quiet stare she made more hazy, folkloric and mythical all rumours of occultation about her.

Often Tankia, son of the village tout Chakrapani, came to see Kunti with someone or other. A whisper was going on about the reason of his visits: Chakrapani is conspiring to make Tankia the adopted son of Kunti so that he can grab her property free. One day Chakrapani's wife, that is mother of Tankia, could not bear this anymore. She set upon a long and tortuous harangue with her husband: "Oh my god! You are a raving lunatic. You keep with yourself your love for wealth. Keep with yourself love for your son and your wife. If you send my son to that vampire another time, remember, I will abandon you and go away. You emasculated dud, listen, one can get any number of men to sleep with, but not another son."

Chakrapani was the tout and go-getter in ten villages where he settled miscellaneous disputes through mediation and he was not one who would abandon this so easily just because his wife said this. He took cheap local liquor in a hooch shop until he was thoroughly drunk. He cursed Kunti until he remembered his wife, then he cursed his wife until something strange happened to him. He slumped there, crawled on his palms and knees, and rambled as if he was possessed by a ghost: Whoa! Hey! What is this in front of me? What is this colour on your face? Is this the colour which lights the sacrificial and sacred wood-fire when ghee is poured on it? Whoa, why am I slipping beneath your feet? Whoa, your feet have grown into the soil like roots. Alas, I have fallen here clinging to earth with my teeth, the soil tastes like the elixir of immortality, amrita, amrita, amrita.

If someone says that after this episode Chakrapani was transformed to a good human being, that would be false and exaggerated. But he never spoke a word about Kunti again after this day.

It was decided by the residents of the settlement that a *jatra* will be performed there. This is an open theatre drama, with plenty of music and plots, performed from late evening till dawn. In their old village there was a proper theatre troupe. There was an aphorism that someone in Ankamara, who could not perform in any way in the theatre was not eligible to become an employee in the landlord's house or farm land. In Ankamara, there was a proper permanent stage made of stones, bricks and lime mortar. There was a large field in front of the stage for audience. At the end of the field, there was a large high narrow platform, also made of lime mortar and bricks, for female audience, including recently wed daughters-in-law, who wanted to sit separately. In the new settlement there was neither a stage for the actors nor a field for the audience; but before any effort was made in this direction the decision to stage a play had been taken.

There was a large array of white boulders on the backside of the village. The rehearsal for the opera was held here. The boulders were good for thrones and chairs, but when the sun rose high, they became blazing hot. Children of the settlement, who were without clothes now and carried smaller children without clothes on their waists, gathered there to watch the rehearsal. Old people who had learnt original opera from original masters discussed between themselves the performance in whispers with great seriousness and grave faces, but did not say anything aloud.

When an overweight Gandhari told a Duryodhan who had butterfly moustache and combed his oiled hair to a smooth and sticky cover on his head: 'O prince! Do not procrastinate anymore. Behold, in front of you there is Kurukshetra, the Dharmakshetra, the place where righteousness is to be re-established. Proceed with your obligation to duty, so that the Umbrella party is wiped out from the breast of earth...'

At this moment, Chandara's son Markand, father of seven living and four dead children and village level secretary of Umbrella party, was coming out of his house trying to wear his crumpled shirt stained with cow dung. His wife came out of his house swearing: 'Where are you going in shirt and dhoti like a prince? Will you not go to harvesting of paddy for your wages? Who has stacked food for you in the house?'

Markand had seen that there was enough rice for today, so there will be no calamity today, and without answering his wife walked on wondering which beat or *taal* in the *mridangam* will go with the dialogue when the words Umbrella party reached his ears and he stood still with shock, forgot to breathe and panted.

'I will take care of you one by one,' Markand muttered as he walked on.

Duryodhan had drunk two rupees' worth hooch from Rain party and experienced the feeling of arrogance and loyalty worth two hundred thousand rupees. He left the Pandavas and his other enemies, came near Markand, slapped him hard without a word and some teeth fell on the ground. Duryodhan looked at the ground and then Markand's mouth for blood to come out. Blood did not come out. The teeth were artificial, not original. During the last general election to the State legislature,

Markand had collected the cost of a set of teeth from Umbrella party.

Markand gathered the teeth, ran to Kunti's house and knocked her door.

After a long time, the door opened a little. A face appeared, almost made of wood.

'I am Markand, Chandara's son Markand,' Markand said.

Kunti did not say anything. Markand narrated: this happened, that happened.

'I am an old woman. Why are you dragging me into all this?' Kunti said. She went inside her house, leaving the front door ajar. Markand was gripped with a sudden unknown fear like a child, and he scurried away.

Kunti came back, bolted the door and returned to her bedroom to lie down on her bed. She saw Govind, wearing a paper crown, sitting on her cot. The brown thread on one side of the crown had loosened and the crown had crumpled to that side. He sat cross-legged, his belly bulged over his lap, and he smiled showing his betel-stained teeth. His smile showed that he was not sure of the kind of reception he will get.

'Are you angry?' Govind asked in a nasalized voice. 'I could not help you with your problem, after all.'

Kunti giggled like an adolescent girl. What could she do with such silly stupidity other than laugh?

She stopped laughing. She said in a voice without emotions: 'After returning from your office, I resigned from my job, so do not show me your bravado. I did everything for you. You loved Sundari and you played with me. When you were slapped and fell down in the paddy field, my mother helped to pick you up. I was happy that you came. I was sad to see the state you were in. Ma sprinkled water on your forehead and made you smell rock salt. I made your bed in the barn house.'

She continued with the same voice: 'In the night, after taking food, I showed that I was going out to wash my hands, and I stepped over the imaginary ancient tall doors of generations which restricted our freedom. I opened the bamboo-frame gate of the barn, entered, crossed stacks of dry paddy plants. My chest reverberated as if a country paddy-thresher was pounding and separating rice from paddy on it. I was worried: if you send me back, if you ask me why I have come to you! If you ask: don't I know that I, my family, my clan, all land holders are your enemy?

'I must have gently touched the door of the barn house, you opened the door, as if you were waiting. I became unnerved, looked back and saw the clear moon. I did not have any faith anymore in the courage which had brought me here. Someone or other must have seen me coming here. But I was defiant, which kind of fear could have separated me from you that night?

'The moon was crazy, what kind of wacky madness had possessed it?

'I did not know whether I was at your feet or you were at my feet. I was shivering with the memory of a cold and helpless moonlight. I said, will you leave me here? My sari is slipping down, dirt sticks to the redundant hand-woven designer cotton sari, the dirt of inability to atone throughout life for the sins of that night.

'You did not budge, I could not understand what happened to you, you lay crumpled like a brown centipede coiled around itself, on the bur-reed mat on the ground. I pushed you, rolled you over. I asked you, if you do not have the masculinity to love, why did you call me? You did not reply at all. I asked, shall I wear my clothes? Even then, you remained silent. I put on my sari and ran back to our home. I was so ugly, so unattractive, so dispensable, so unworthy of you!

'You will never know what harm you caused to me, what you broke inside me. I could have become anything in my life, anything I wanted and happily too. I could have smashed the shackles of one stage of my life and climbed over to another stage. But before I faced a test for each elevation, before I put out my first step for each migration, a sad and indignant disappointment flowed and permeated inside my body. Even my bones and their interiors shivered in the cold frost outside. I knew that I am not capable of anything. In that moonlit night, as I returned carrying the burden of lifelong humiliation, the experience remained with me for ever. I remained stunted with this burden, and you are responsible for this.'

Kunti was excited and angry with this long recollection. Govind was not offended or perturbed. He was never offended or perturbed. He smiled innocently. He said in the same nasalized voice: 'You were so small that day dear girl. What unredeemable sins I was about to commit that night!'

Kunti became pacified in a moment. Since many days ago, she had lost every ability to believe anything against Govind.

After some time, Govind pretended to be busy and left. Kunti had her menopause from that month. Throughout that night, when she realized at the age of forty-two, that she had menopause, she became soaked with an unprecedented sacred desire. The sacredness on bamboo support of the thatched roof, the straw, the gossamer was transparent like shining dew drops on grass in autumn mornings. The odour of rusted iron which had pervaded her house for some years disappeared suddenly. The heat and dust in the air subsided and from somewhere the fragrance of wild flowers resembling the fragrance of fresh honey filled up the house. The villagers in the settlement colony wondered why the spring had arrived before its time.

Kunti experienced something with absolute clarity. She is a child and listening to an old story on the veranda of the ashram of Alekh sanyasi. In the story, the king was extremely lazy and obese, suffered from almost every disease mentioned in the *Charak Samhita,* the treatise on Indian Ayurveda. From his throne, he had ordered beheading of many doctors of Ayurveda as they failed to cure him of his illness. (The veranda of Alekh sanyasi was high. In his garden, there were three deer and innumerable butterflies.) The worried king went to a hermit who resembled Alekh sanyasi. The hermit gifted a deer to the king and asked the king to run after the deer for the whole day, every day. Kunti can know with absolute clarity that the king was actually Govind and Kunti was the deer who was running ahead of him.

SIX

Those days, Kunti was occasionally coming out of her house for a short time. She particularly went to religious fairs, festivals where offerings were made to gods and goddesses through the God of Fire, and mass-worships and rites where the devoted went into trance possessed by deities; yet, despite her presence in all these venues, she remained detached, as if a hallowed ladder of miraculous esotericism elevated and isolated her. In front of a sacrificial fire ritual she would sit equipoise, tranquil, as though she were meditating, did not say a word, yet carrying out, with a certain resigned irony, the little instructions from the Brahmin priest who rode a bicycle to reach the venue of worship, like: fill the sanctified pot with water, dip the strand of creeper grass in the ghee and sprinkle ghee into the fire, join your palms to offer namaskar to the flames, and so on. Her face would be ablaze with the light from crimson flames that curled upwards into smoke and nothingness.

'Do not sit so close to the fire, dear,' her Ma told her one day during a ritual. (Kunti had observed a twelve-month-long mourning ritual for her mother. Her logic was: the practice of the twelve-day rites is the condensed form of the original twelve month long mourning rites). Kunti was startled and looked around to see her mother; her mother's face was going hazy.

The Brahmin who used to come on a bicycle asked: 'For whom did you supplicate, daughter?'

'The deity knows it,' Kunti said, and saw that Ma had gone away.

'Will you burn some more ghee in the sacrificial fire?' the Brahmin asked.

Kunti looked at the bronze bowl containing the ghee. 'No,' she said, still seated by the altar, absent minded. The fire died away, leaving behind blazing embers.

'Give me leave to go, daughter,' the priest said, 'because I have to perform a morning worship ritual in the moneylender's house tomorrow.'

'There won't be any puja in their house tomorrow,' Kunti said. 'There will be a baby born to the family, and they will be polluted.'

Moonlight washes her face. The embers die away to ashes. Seated on the grey-coloured ground, in the shower of moonlight, Kunti looks old. Her face looks hazy, her clean white clothes appear somewhat soiled. The priest would not ask how she knew that a baby would be born to the moneylender's the next day.

One day Nathu Mahalik, age forty-five, profession cultivation, domicile his own village, an infamous shirker as a farmhand, one who knew how to play the mridanga and sing – tried to humour Kunti: 'Here, sister, it's so good that you came back.'

'So you all had been waiting for me!' replied Kunti.

'Dear sister, how does it matter if someone waits for you or does not? The soil will surely beckon you enough some day, you will surely return to it.'

'Don't teach me those thick profundities. All my life I have been a teacher and I have grown old now.'

'Sister dear, I am illiterate and ignorant, how can I teach you? I was just adding adages to words to make the conversation. Do not get angry. May I ask you something, from where did you acquire this divine power? With which guru did you take your initiation?'

'Hey, does not your sister live in the neighbouring village, across the paddy lands? You rush there, fast,' she said and retreated into her house.

Nathu was a proper moron. He ran straight to his sister's house. His wife was yelling: 'Come on, the rice is served, have your food first.' But he was in no mood to relent. When he reached his sister's house he saw her family was in the midst of a violent fight relating to land, his brother-in-law had been overpowered and encircled by the members of the opposite group, defenseless, with no one to come to his rescue. Nathu ran near him and pulled him out from the crowd; it was matter of seconds before a catastrophic bloodshed. The crowd more out of surprise than anything else, broke up, and then returned to their senses.

The same day, at about noon, or maybe before noon, a skinny, gaunt-looking man in clean, pressed pants and shirt reached the village riding a rickety bicycle. That he was not a native was writ large all over his looks that displayed confidence, indifference, and elegance, and each step he trod imprinted on the backdrop he had been leaving behind this fact that he was a stranger to the village. He had hair like curls of thin metal wires that immediately caught the attention of Dhushi, the old woman, who was in the habit of jabbering nonsense incessantly to herself, and she recited a rhyme:

Ha, a baldy from somewhere

On his head not a strand of hair

Only loads of soot and cobweb to wear;

He has sneaked into someone's kitchen,

Or, this head of his

Makunda, the barber, has not surely seen.

Then the old woman blabbered on and on about Makunda, the recalcitrant barber and then left for the low-lying lands. The stranger was nervous from the beginning, his nervousness aggravated after the incident with the old woman. He fumbled and stammered as he asked a small boy: 'Could you tell me where the one who has come to your village recently stays?' (The stranger, through his query, had swallowed his spit a few times, missed a few phonemes and bungled with the subject-verb agreement.)

The boy was puzzled, even shocked with the abstract question; he walked backwards for a while, broke into loud uncontrollable bawl and swallowed a large lump of his snot. Another boy passed the stranger rolling a rusted bicycle rim. By now the stranger's question, like a sparrow, hopped and reached: Mr Penga, who was mending a fence on his crop-field at a close distance; the sixteen-year-old plump, fair as white marble, youngest daughter-in-law of the village moneylender, who was a mother of a dead and a living child and who was now flattening cow-dung cakes which will be used as fuel in the hearth; Chandrabhanu, who had been a driver wearing trousers, but now a tout wearing dhoti-kurta, in anticipation of his political career as a head of the local self government, practicing the art of a professional tout; and then flew away. All the listeners noticed the man and his question. They swarmed around the unexpected stranger. A couple of females, from their verandahs, quietly scanned the stranger in their mind in all possible details; perhaps this alien magician at their disposal would fish out from his magic handkerchief, and exhibit for all, the enchanting pigeon that held the secrets to Kunti's past including her ancient love affairs!

Chandrabhanu was the cleverest in the audience. (When he was a child, his father had left their home to become a monk. They too lost their lands in the dam and when the compensation money was being distributed, Chandrabhanu came back to ask for his share. The litigation for compensation money had not been resolved when he came to the new settlement. There, he encroached upon some land in the housing area by his might and befitting his calibre. In any case most of the land in housing area had been occupied by the displaced people through mutual consent as this was not allotted properly and people believed that there was thus no justice in the legal process. Because the rule of the jungle justifies that you claim territories according to your might. For such reasons, no one in Ankamara settlement had respect for the law.)

Everyone including Chandrabhanu got baffled although they knew very well where Kunti's house was, and that the stranger, surely, was asking about her. Everyone lost his reason, except Penga; he was not intelligent enough to have reason, so there was no question of his losing it, and he showed the stranger the way to Kunti's house.

To continue about Penga, the least said about his silliness the better. Once, a cow of theirs died in the cowshed still tethered to the pole. That meant the cow would not attain liberation of the soul, and this is considered a terrible sin for Penga who had tethered the cow; but who explains sin to an idiot? Later the cow's spirit entered his three-year-old daughter. Four months thus passed, after which only Penga sent for the sorcerer. 'Why couldn't you send for me earlier?' the infuriated sorcerer snapped at him.

'We thought,' Penga, the blockhead said, 'she too will start giving milk. If the cow's spirit is inside her body, why should not she give milk?'

Since that day, Penga's daughter, only three years old, would not come out to the street out of embarrassment. She has been married since ages now, yet whenever she visited her parents' home, the boys of the village teased her and her family members questioned the parentage of these rowdy boys.

The stranger rested his bicycle against the veranda of Kunti's house, and clattered the iron rings on the door. Kunti came out immediately, as if she had been awaiting someone's arrival. A huge crowd had gathered on the street in front of her house; where did such a large mass of people come from? They looked eager, optimistic and excited; perhaps this queer alien could connect Kunti's strange and perhaps transcendent world to their banal and fallen world.

Their resolute breath was sucking away every molecule of oxygen from the atmosphere and the thatched roof of the house wobbled with the effect. Some straw of the thatch fluttered away. The people are not howling any longer; they now talk in whispers; a faint tune unrolls slowly, as if a thousand and more bumblebees are humming at a little distance up at the place where human voice can reach from Kunti's house. In the sharp eagerness of the assemblage, the curly tufts of hair of the stranger quiver.

'It is me,' the stranger said. 'Bhanu.'

Kunti is surprised. She fetched a palm-leaf mat from her house and said: 'Sit here.'

Bhanu acquiesced that what he was envisioning with his opened eyes was no more the reality; because he saw Kunti standing before him, yet he did not quite see her. It was only a summer cloud, a cloud enshrined by flashes of lightening – alternating between too much illumination, and too much darkness.

*****

The first time Bhanu had met Kunti, he had not grown a moustache or beard and in that adolescent life of his, bracketed between studies-home-football-home, Kunti hogged many a role: mother to a one-year-old toddler, the last resort of a seventeen year old, highly sensitive adolescent; or the lyrics of a song looking for a tune in the desolate dark den of ghosts and hobgoblins and going crazy. Kunti was working in a school where Bhanu's unmarried elder sister too taught. They were put up in a mess, along with another music teacher who was blind. The music teacher had become blind on an occasion, when as a child she had suffered from hookworms in her stomach and conjunctivitis of the eyes, and had swapped the medication; she swallowed the eye-drops and put the drug for the worms in her eyes, and had lost her eyesight. Since Bhanu knew that he was not born to be a scholar, and his father's business was expanding, he gave up his studies with the alibi that he was helping in his father's business (and gave up the domain of business for his studies) and often came to that tiny town to brag as it suited his age.

About Kunti, Bhanu did not know much. Except for

a few impressions, like: Kunti, a golden coloured wrist watch on a thin, too thin, dust-coloured wrist where many veins showed; a precious smile rare as an oasis in a desert, a cuckoo's song resonating by the banks of a spring thin-as-a-little-finger in a leafy woods – Bhanu did not have any other elaborate knowledge about Kunti. Everyday, everywhere, an emerald river of the moonlit night flowed about and there were unceasing assaults of fragrances from blossoming trees.

The first day he had come to Kunti's town, he had had a scuffle with one of the passengers in the bus he was travelling in. It was a small issue that the scuffle had ensued from, but his lips ruptured and bled. On the way to Kunti's mess he had toyed with the idea that he would return to his town, collect a few friendly goons and return for revenge. He analyzed the feasibility of the plan thoroughly, decided that it was not feasible, and went and reached at his elder sister's mess with bleeding lips, carrying along the loads of his unredeemed mutilated ego.

By then, Kunti, having looked for someone before whom she could have poured out her heart, having pined for long and with intense earnestness for nobody in particular, and not finding any one good enough, had become almost desperately hopeless. She had begun to hate all men. She could not have shared with her colleagues how Govind had betrayed her (Govind's betrayal had zoomed larger and more savage in her mind over these years), nor her inexplicable hatred for men, and hence she talked very little. For the last few days, for about a month now, she was taking mild sleep-inducing pills. At times the thought struck her that she would perhaps be admitted to a mental asylum, and this idea was solacing; because in a mental asylum she could do anything that she would want to; like, she could throw banana skins everywhere, bray, throw dirty gestures at doctors, and above all could shout at others all the four lettered words she knew from her childhood, but which she had never uttered as she was a "good" child with good upbringing. In a mental hospital she could even take off her clothes and jump around half-naked before men and women, as they show it in movies.

After the scuffle in the bus, when Bhanu reached his sister's mess she was not there. Kunti gathered him up gently. He spent eight days in her mess and enjoyed the most romantic recovery of his life, and became Kunti's own. He found her closer to him than his own sister. And the two women started to have sniffs and sobs among themselves. Every time Bhanu left the mess, his elder sister looked relatively relieved, while Kunti's eyes welled. The next time Bhanu came, he slept with his head on Kunti's lap and later, in his sleep, put his hands over her. The following morning Kunti, narrating the incident, rolled in laughter; while Bhanu quietened his adolescent's hunger and broke down. As if to atone for this, the next day when Kunti left for her school, he had a long stroll, under a scorching sun, and returned like a blackened burnt out log after Kunti had returned from school, and asked her: 'Why did you laugh at me in the morning? I am a kid, believe me.'

Kunti was frightened. That night, to prove that he still had not grown, he slept in Kunti's bed resting his head on her bosom. Inside Bhanu a huge blind and obstinate reptile was stirring slowly from under a deep heap of hay and dry leaves; and Kunti could laugh at him no more. 'My chest is hurting,' she said and removed his head gently. He slept away from her.

In the middle of the night he again woke up, and slept next to Kunti, his head hugging her feet and whispered hoarsely, 'Believe me, I am a little boy, I have not grown up.'

Kunti is blissfully in the middle of a slumber, a summer moon glides by outside the tiny window of the adobe-house. A night bird is announcing itself somewhere, perhaps an owl. Kunti's sari slips away off her summer-bare bosom; she wears no bodice nor bra, her perfect hemispherical breasts radiate a warm aroma that spreads to her face, wrapping it with smoke.

Bhanu turned away towards the wall in fear and fell asleep, and dreamt throughout the night: Kunti had left by train for some unknown destination. He was running towards the railway station, his shorts, loosened at the waist, slipping down his waist time and again; and the moment he reached the railway station, the train had rolled away from the platform solemnly, and unconcerned.

About two or three years later Kunti got a teaching job in a government run school, and she left her job at that privately managed school. And along with it, that little town where green paddy fields stretched in every direction, and which had the pastoral silence of a village. After she left, Bhanu had come once and saw her in a white sari fleeing away outside the old mess of adobe-house over a thick carpet of mango leaves. He ran to the place where he had seen her, a lone dry leaf was quivering in the wind there only.

Five years after this incident, Kunti was transferred to Bhadrak, Bhanu's town. Bhanu had grown in years, and thought himself as the sun since the day an astrologer, consulting the *Bhrigusamhita*, had told him that he was a revolutionary in his last life and had been executed for the same cause. He continued to be the skipper of the school soccer team, his father had cancer of the scrotum and his business that had more and more competitors was stuck more often than it grew. His hair was now growing into the shade of ash, and all the bachelors who were of an age that they could have married his elder sister had forsaken the world.

Kunti, in the meantime, trying to keep herself engaged with literature, culinary arts, religious institutions, and not finding these of interest, had got herself occupied in small drudgeries, such as teaching, hassles of students and envy of colleagues, the harassing school managing committee and inevitable touts. Seeing Bhanu, she tidied up herself, put moisturizer on her face and powdered it, though she felt bashful and apprehensive now that Bhanu had grown bigger. Bhanu's old crush for her, which had been like a buoyant cloud, had become condensed by now. Though his business was getting stuck up everywhere, with the Land Officer for land, at the bank for capital, and for electricity, water connection and share capital, he treated people with his cracking guffaws. Occasionally he dreamt in nights that he, after a lot of careful maneuvring, had brought Kunti to a hut in a deep forest but had ejaculated before she was undressed.

Yet he came to visit her regularly; and every time as he returned from her, used to wonder: 'Why had I come here?'

***

Kunti came out of the house. She was carrying buttermilk, and on her face the same old incredulous surprise; as if Bhanu was saying: 'I have not grown old, believe me, I am still a kid.' Kunti kept the tumbler on the ground, at a distance from Bhanu, and said: 'Drink.'

Outside, in the collective exhalations of the crowd, a whirlwind ghost was taking wings.

In grieved silence Bhanu asked: 'Am I polluted, and not to be touched?'

'No,' said Kunti, 'I am polluted, I haven't changed into fresh and washed clothes.'

Bhanu lifted the tumbler to drink. The coalesced thirsty breath of the onlookers sucked away the liquid in the glass, drying it, its bottom was sucked up, inwards.

An exquisite kaleidoscope of crystals and coloured stones pops up with a sudden noise inside Bhanu's mind and then crackles; a beam of clean white sunshine remains concentrated there. He rises to his feet, puzzled, can he kiss the torn plastic slippers of Kunti again, like he used to do and can he lapse into tears while doing so?

A fear gripped him and he pushed through the crowd, fleeing out of the village, while he could hear Kunti, who was perhaps calling out to him: *come, come back, leap back to me my little calf.*

He heard it, pretended that he hadn't and pedalled away hurriedly, though not knowing why he should be so much frightened and of what, or why he should scamper away and from where.

SEVEN

Kunti had always blamed her mother for every blameworthy occurrence, since her childhood. When she came to live in the hostel and had to serve food for herself, she sobbed through her nose and blamed her mother every time she took her hand to her mouth. Her father was alive, but she did not blame him. Those were days past long ago, now she did not feel her stomach half-filled when she served herself a meal.

Those were the days when her mother used to visit Kunti in her hostel bringing with her pickles, *ber* berries, sun-dried black-gram patties, and from their back yard garden vegetables and sturdy spinach stems. When Kunti went home during vacations, she too took with her glucose packets, vitamin and mineral tonics for Ma and babies, and dhotis for her brothers. Her elder brothers, by then, had their worlds revolve round their wives and flaunted a new vanity and arrogance. The husband of her elder sister was scraping out a livelihood in Calcutta, was taking opium for his tuberculosis and did not indulge in banters and romantic jokes with Kunti, the younger sister of his wife with whom he could do this. For pretty many days Kunti, during her home visits, would bathe her younger brother Gobara, undressing him completely. One summer vacation she realized that she could no longer bathe Gobara and she went so mad that she spent the entire vacation punishing him for any little slips of his, boxing his ears, and slapping him hard on his cheeks.

After the holidays were over and she was back in the school, she discovered that she had been tangled in a deeper bond with him, more than that of a brother. Her menstrual periods had started three years earlier and she could no longer confide anything in Gobara, and for that too she blamed her mother out of habit.

One day Ma told her: 'You were so blinded with your ego, pointing a mocking finger at every bride who came to or went out from the village, that god could not bear with it, and did not wish to see you as a bride.'

'It's all your fault,' Kunti snapped back, 'because you gave birth to me I have to endure so much pain, for so long.'

Kunti never blamed her father; as if because he had died so early in life, his culpability had withered away.

Kunti, with her trails of grumbles, nagging, upbraiding, was torturing Ma's life. On some days she would be really nasty with her Ma, her charades would be so incising that the most perseverant person on earth would melt into berry sized tear drops in no time. Ma never shed a tear before Kunti; she listened to all her whinges and tantrums and when she was really hurt and shattered with her daughter's accusations she would cry quietly, alone, and her tears would continue flowing down for several silent hours.

Once when Kunti had received an urgent letter from Bhanu asking her to come to his city (Kunti had not been transferred to the city where Bhanu was staying then), she took the last bus in the evening, all by herself, gripped by a fear that Bhanu was in some danger. It was dark by the time the bus reached the city.

After getting off the bus, she took a cycle-rickshaw. The rickshaw puller asked the details of the destination, and the route they must take, stressing every word of his questions, and Kunti fumbled for a definite, detailed answer. The man took his rickshaw away from the town, towards a desolate stretch. Kunti was aware that the rickshaw-puller was taking a wrong route, hijacking her, she almost shouted, but was stopped by a sense of shame – what if the rickshaw was on the right route? And everyone would think that she was an uninformed clodhopping dunderhead. She hated herself and began missing her childhood days: how good were those days when she could say aloud anything she wanted to!

The town was left behind. She was gripped by the fear that she would be raped by the rickshaw-puller inevitably, but she could not open her mouth. This fear was complex, like a picture with minute details, terror and loneliness arrived hand in hand and engulfed her. Before her the sand and the thick woods stretched for ever towards the confluence of two rivers. Kunti screamed with a force that almost tore apart her body, and her sobs and tears disappeared into her tearing wail. A gentleman, with a set of pearl-like teeth, whose looks said he had been moulded from atoms and molecules of suavity and urbanity, came to rescue her. He gave two slaps to the rickshaw-puller and rode alongside the rickshaw on his motor bike. After a distance a police officer in uniform reached there (who, in fact, looked like a rapist). As soon as the gentleman saw the police officer, he sped away on his motor cycle.

'Do not ever commit such mistake again,' Makara, the

son of Shambhu cautioned her. (Makara was from Kunti's village Ankamara. His father Shambhu was a jolly good fellow – I will tell you about him some other time.)

Kunti was taken aback over the whole incident, but what startled her most was: why did not Makara chase that rogue?

'I am posted as a police sub-inspector out here,' said Makara. 'That man is a criminal, he is the president of the ruling political party for the district; he was on his way to rape you. There was a news a few days ago, a much-hyped news. You must have read about a rape case in this locality a few days ago. This man is the culprit; he was acquitted in the higher court. Nowadays we do not wield any authority in matters of crime any more. We cannot control or prevent any crime.'

Kunti was not perturbed over the irresponsibility or impotence of the legal system. She was disturbed over something eternally incomplete and irreversible: when she would be dead, all her virtues and vices would come to an end too. But the sins she had been saved from, from Govind, from Bhanu and from that sophisticated rapist, such sins those were committed by Sundari and those not committed by Kunti, such sins those were prevented by Makara – would come to an end too; yet she was saved of something, an experience that would have been beyond the matrix of virtues and vices, unconnected with them, something that she would never have, a torture and terror that she would never feel, and never forget. This not-being was exclusively her own, as she had no more faith in anything beyond death, and particularly when the giving-and-taking of this life has been over, when all debts have been settled, what could she expect and with whose help and care, in a world where all relationships were merely settlement of debts? Not even one miracle occurred in the life she had lived so far, so for another life that could have miracle makers near her, whose existence she suspects, suspects completely, why should she wait? What would it mean if that night, beneath a light drizzle, amidst the sands and shrubs, she had been raped, mist blowing from the rivers, she, dreadful and shameful and disgraced, struggling against suffering from indescribable physical and mental violence, would have carried through her life the ghastly burden of life-long horror, shame and tears, which she did not deserve, what and whose purpose would it serve; but is shown as so routine and prevalent in Hindi films?

When Kunti returned carrying on her shoulders the outrage of her could-have-happened rape, like every other time she blamed her mother for this. Ma was staying in the village. When she came to Kunti, she would stay for a day or a half and would be restless to rush back to the village. A terrible shapeless rumour made rounds that the village was going to be submerged, and Ma would say, suppose she stayed longer, and the village submerged while she was away, what would happen to her house, and the cows and the utensils and the deities and the paddy and abracadabra? Ma had a premonition that Kunti was going to face some danger (mothers always know such things and they alone know how) and offered vows and prayers before the village deity, whose life's years were running out with the forthcoming river dam, and she wept alone and silently. The whole of next day she shouted abuses and curses at her sons and their wives, throughout the night she repented for having cursed and blamed them and she blamed Kunti the whole of the following day because she had upbraided her sons for no fault of theirs. She told her: *it is because of you that*

I cursed my sons, you are a girl with inauspicious influence, and called her more names. In the night she became sad again, and cried alone because she had cursed her poor lonesome unfortunate daughter so much.

When the village was actually submerged, neither the mother nor the sons went to live in the new settlement, put up by the government. They sold off their shares and moved to the town, or somewhere without an address and became like gypsies. (Kunti's share remained unsold and unoccupied.) Mother became demented, she was reduced to an incessant rambler; her body skeletal and her mind an infertile hard rocky field. She thinned away like a reed, and her bones knocked when she walked or when she moved her limbs. Kunti's eldest brother migrated to the nearby town, and with his gold-nosed wife and three cute children, pretty as red-velvet-beetles, settled down peacefully in a slum on the outskirts in a shanty made of rags, tin-sheets and sack-cloth. He had taken, towards his share, their beautifully carved twin-leafed door that had metal knobs on it, which belonged to the common possessions of the family; but till the end of this tale he had not been able to build a house where that door could have sat aesthetically. They had used the door to cover the sewerage drain that flowed in front of their shack.

After the village was submerged Ma never came to Kunti again, as if the village was their only bondage. When she had come to Kunti for the last time, Ma had brought for her a piece of root that was for invigorating youth. But Ma lied to her that the root was a cure for Kunti's hemorrhoid. When Kunti wore the root, tying it on her hand, above the elbow, she felt her feet and palms going pink with flushes of a new flow of blood, the oblique warmth of which heated her whole body and excited her heart. Then Kunti became religious thoroughly, she filled her life with silent evening prayers at some religious institution, and with chanting of hymns and meditation and perambulating the town early in the mornings, on Fridays and Tuesdays, singing aloud *bhajan*, with the religious group, and she gave up these rituals after a year, less disappointed and more bored, and became hopeless and irreligious once more.

In these years Gobara had gone off to faraway Assam. Before leaving he had come to Kunti to collect his travel expenses and expenditure for a month, and many a parting scene were enacted when he left.

(Bhanu had come two days later. Kunti was all praises for Gobara, from the nails on his toes to the hair on his head. Bhanu said: 'Gobara will not return home, to Odisha, anymore; he will marry someone in that part and settle down.'

'Do not have such thoughts, everyone is not like you,' Kunti had retorted.)

Kunti had hurriedly bought for Gobara woolen socks, and had cooked dinner for him taking culinary tips from magazines for women. In the night she confided in her Ma how rude her headmistress had been to her, and the way she talked to Kunti as if the she was throwing the words at Kunti, how she had been rescued from a probable rape, and about the painful cramps in her stomach during the periods. Ma too narrated her malicious and uncouth daughters-in-law, the latest, still fresh gossip from their village, the sciatica pain in her back and stubborn bowels. Kunti felt sheltered at once, again. Her hands no more stretched out to emptiness, a firm assurance appeared where ever her hands reached out.

'You know Ma, I always blame you in all the bad times of mine,' she said through her sobs.

Ma said: 'What else are mothers for? That's why I am your ma.'

Kunti said: 'Ma dear, I was in love with Govind; had he not been a lumpen, I would have married him.'

Ma said: 'Dear, Markand was saying Govind has kept a portly school teacher as his mistress.'

'Papa should have lived longer,' Kunti said. 'Things would have been better.'

'Your father was a good-for-nothing fellow,' Ma said. 'He could not fend even for me, leave alone my children.'

'Oh no, do not talk like that,' Kunti snapped. 'You will fall into hell.'

Ma heard the voice of father and she became quiet.

By the time the village went under water, mother had become a complete wreck, and very old. Then she did not talk for three or four continuous days together, and then went on and on for days; as though she would die in a while and must exhaust her reservoir of what she had wanted to say, but had not said. But she spoke so fast, and in such hurry, that her speech was unintelligible, resembling ramblings.

Ma visited Kunti many days after the daughter had returned to the settlement. Ma was almost blind then and had become deaf like a wall. She ran her fingers through Kunti's body, feeling her from her head down to her legs and spoke through her nostrils, in her country tongue:

'How come your skin feels soft like the feathers of a heron, dear?'

(Long ago, Ma had a yellow coloured sari, an Odisha silk of the yarn-dyed Sonepur weave. She looked beautiful and gorgeous, like goddess Lakshmi, in that sari though she had been a mother of five children by then. Kunti used to borrow that sari from her for special occasions, drape herself in it and wonder at her reflection in the mirror on the mud-wall: *why don't I look pretty like Ma even if I am studying myself in the mirror so minutely?*) She felt ticklish all over when Ma touched her. In fact she was ticklish ever since she was a child, and this ticklishness never left her.

Ma had become almost dumb. While walking she made the noise of a bundle of sticks. She looked like a grasshopper while squatting. She was trying to establish a link with her daughter in that muteness; but Kunti had migrated away above all these relationships. She was elevated to another expanse from where she could see a coloured, lighted path in her front, and a stuffed gloom in the stretch behind; and she could not return and re-establish an affiliation again. One morning Ma evaporated into the void the way she had come, with the noise of a bundle of sticks. As she was departing, all the woodpeckers of the village started pecking at trees in a chorus and the noise of the bundle of sticks of mother going away was lost among the rhythmic sound of woodpeckers. Therefore, no one could make out that she had left.

After Ma left, Kunti became so buoyant that she had to hang the load of a bundle of granite pebbles from her sari end, and to carry her whole life's collective memories on her head; otherwise she would have flown off. Save for the inexplicable fear of being weightless, Kunti had become completely composed and tranquil. But she had become absolutely uncommunicative and wordless. She could presage every event, she had answers on the tip of her tongue to every unpronounced question, and she knew too that every answer and every statement of hers was redundant and irrelevant. She had reached the stratum where articulation was superfluous. In fact every form of sound was an aberration there, since the most important and the most pragmatic are communicated only through silence.

EIGHT

When she had returned to the settlement, Kunti had had a faith that though the settlement has been rendered rootless, deformed and handicapped now, somehow it will surely salvage her from desolation, abandonment, and consequential death, though she made no effort from her side for seeking such protection. Those days she was often angry with the Gods and Goddesses and had become like a child.

Those days she spoke to Gods and Goddesses alone like a child: 'You see God, do not be angry with me. Please God, have I not helped anyone in my life who needed help? (Then, every time, she made a list of the people she had helped.) Do not scare me.'

And Kunti was becoming ancient without anyone knowing about this. Anyone who was conscious of time could have realized her increasing retrogression to ancientness; but in that makeshift settlement, culture and civilization was nascent and almost nonexistent and no one could notice this change in Kunti.

A man named Nakhia alias Niyati worked in the irrigation project not very far from the settlement. He had played the role of "Fate" in village opera, and that is how he got this second name Niyati, and that is how since those days it was his habit to recite and explain gnomes. One morning Kunti looked for Niyati and could not find him. She found her son and told him: 'Look, tell your father not to go to work without informing me.'

Before the son could say anything to his father, Niyati had gone to work on his bicycle and was stuck between two moving trucks and he remembered a gnome, which meant, when two elephants fight, the poor grass suffers the pain. This gnome was the last gnome in his life, he did not recite another gnome in his life, never again, because he was squeezed between the two trucks and died. It is not necessary to reveal that some people blamed Kunti for this and asked Chakrapani to take care of the matter. Chakrapani, who knew everything about land and mundane matters of the world, and could create problems relating to them when he wished (so that he can solve them later) did not get into matters relating to Kunti out of fear. In any case, Kunti came out of her house rarely, had no interest in getting into the affairs of others, and had become like an impersonal institution. Her childhood, youth and mundane life had disappeared from the memory of villagers, and even from the memory of Kunti.

One year, during the winter month of Magha, a surprising southern wind blew in. The wind was calm and gentle. But the wind also pushed people to a mild awareness that each person had lost something, but he or she could not remember what had been lost. The wind swayed the loose straw of the lower edge of the thatch in the courtyard; people had created courtyards by extending the settlement houses built by the government. The coconut trees planted by the people had reached only half their height, and on the leaves sunrays swam down like babies. The one year old hibiscus plant near the shrine of the Village Goddess was laden with red flowers, as if someone had made thick garlands of hibiscus flower and heaped them on the plant. (There was not another flower plant in the whole settlement.) When this strange wind blew, a cold and helpless anxiety, that had no visage, swept through the body of Kunti, as if in a far-off island in an ocean an island has been bombed to dust, an island she has never seen, and will never see; but why and how she hears the heart-rending cries of the residents of that island?

How can I describe the solitude of Kunti? Suppose, you are the sole and autocratic owner of an enormous royal palace. You have no brother, friend, father, husband or any other relation you know of. It is afternoon. You are not waiting for anyone. You are not afraid of anyone. Outside, heavily armed guards are on duty. Inside, the devoted priests and sorcerers have prevented all ghosts and spirits from approaching every spot in the palace. There is utter silence everywhere, even the sound of the flute of the cowherd does not float in because with old age, ulcers and hunger he has forgotten how to play the flute since long ago. Even the royal duties will not require any visitor to come, and you have nowhere to go because you are the princess.

Or suppose, it is an off day, you are an ordinary person, you are waiting all by yourself, someone who is dear to you was to come but did not, nor he has sent any news about himself. All street vendors look like postmen, the gong in the courts of justice sounds like a calling bell in the house, you keep yourself busy with sundry chores and forget that you are waiting for someone; but at some corner of the mind this fact rises and reverberates in the memory. You flip the pages of the newspaper – is your name there? Though why would your name, an ordinary person like you, appear in a newspaper? There is some rustle outside, you go and see. Oh, it is just a breeze. A little later you move the curtain aside and listen to someone calling your name. No, there is not even a bud on the wood-champak tree, somewhere a bird is singing in a mocking voice: go on searching, search, search, search. The night comes. When there is any kind of sound, your ears jerk up, in case someone comes looking for you, does not find you and returns. Through the cracks in the door, you see lumps of darkness moving here and there; there is not anyone else anywhere. The time is perhaps twelve or one AM or two AM; what difference does it make?

Or suppose, tomorrow morning someone dear to you is to leave and go away, you roamed around with your dear one in the cool breeze, you had silly arguments with each other on the fragrance of some wild flower, you had a little picnic in a quaint place, you watched a movie in a theatre, and late in the night you threw childish comments into the darkness. When you bid good night, your dear one asked: 'Will you come to the bus station tomorrow morning?' Because tears would have been such a disgrace now, you smiled and answered: 'Perhaps I will come, if the sleep gives a break.' Though you know that you will not come. Next morning you wake up late because you linger in half sleep. You did this deliberately, because at the bus station you would not have been able to tolerate a farewell to your dear one. It is ten in the morning when you get out of bed. You know that your friend would have left in an early morning bus. You come out, there is a thin banana plant, and lonely sunlight on its leaves. Suddenly you have a hope: often buses do leave late, they are not always punctual. You run and run and run to the bus station. The bus has left at least four hours ago.

Or suppose, you had been born a princess a few thousand years ago, or in the era of Dwapar, when the incarnation of God Krishna had happened. Many heroic men had come to your *swayamvar*, where you were to choose your future husband. The men had come on finest elephants and horses, displaying their valour and power, prosperity and fortune, wit and wisdom. The *swayamvar* was over. A smart prince sneaked to the top through fair and foul means; but your heart stayed back with another person who had been sitting quietly, above the lowly ruckus, who did not let even one word to escape his heart and come to his mouth. He did not say anything, he did not ask for anything, he has not revealed anything; with his incontestable and unassailable shy silence he has pulled your heart strings away. The crowd and noise of *swayamvar* have disappeared, you are continuing to sit on the same throne, you listen to the silence of the departure of this prince, you see the scene of his disappearance, you feel his absence.

One day Bhanu came. He knocked the circular iron knobs of the door. A lock is put through the two circles to lock the house from outside. He had to wait for a long time. Kunti opened the door a little and said from inside the house: 'I know that after I die, you will break the glass of my spectacles, fix dark glasses in its place and wear it as dark glasses. But I will not give you that opportunity. Kunti took off her eyeglasses gently, used a lot of force to break it, smiled, gave it in Bhanu's palms and returned to the interior of her house.

Behind Bhanu the crowd is filled with surprise. He

looked into the darkness of the house and said: 'I am going. I will come some other time. (*That means I will not come again.*)'

Bhanu rolled his bicycle and became discoloured with dust from the hoofs of the crowd behind him. The fragrance of *kadamba* flowers emanate from the broken eyeglasses like the fragrance of sorrow. Bhanu went back rolling his bicycle; he thought that if he rides the cycle and pedals away fast, he will commit another transgression.

Kunti went to her bedroom and saw a smiling Govind sitting on her bed. Kunti saw him but pretended that she has not seen him, went to the deity's room and sat in meditation. Govind felt that he was slapped with insults. He did not come again.

It rained the same afternoon. The white stones of the hillock on the back end of the village were drenched and when the rain stopped the afternoon sunray on the stone made them look like small icebergs. In the evening, Kunti came out of her house and climbed the hillock. The sun was of red and orange colour, and through the clouds a colourful paradise shone clearly. The fresh and expectant glow on her face showed that she could take a few more steps towards the sky and enter paradise. But it was inextricably sad when she reached the top of the hillock: everything around her was sheer gray and the sun had set.

After a few days, it became apparent that no one was looking for Kunti. In a fortnight or a month, someone came to buy paddy, someone came to sell fruits and vegetables which did not grow in the settlement, the local land revenue inspector came to collect annual tax, or the boys of the village came to collect some contribution for the festival of the Village Goddess. Kunti came to know that someone has died. As if death came to the settlement in regular intervals so that the settlement does not become obliterated from the world of news.

In spite of such apparent normalcy, that something unusual will happen could have been known from the colour of the air or the crackling sound of dried palm fronds. The old woman of poor Dasia's house who did not have a son had stopped jabbering and remained quiet. Someone died every one or two months; someone was born every fortnight or month. Jatadhari, when possessed by the Village Goddess, announced when someone was reborn inside the uterus of a woman from the settlement or nearby villages; but of late even illiterate women did not believe him. When the soul of a dead person became a ghost, blood-sucking vampire, or a hungry spirit pining to be released from his limbo through proper obsequies rightfully due to the spirit of an ancestor, the Village Goddess knew. But no one knew well enough if something is going to happen at all in the whole village.

But everyone proposed or expostulated a theory. One day the local land inspector came with a drummer and after a proper beat of drums announced that the rights and title of land given to the displaced people will be formally vested now. The peon of the local self government that is called "Panchayat" came and said that a new law has come into force that from now on, no one will remain poor, in order to make them rich, they will be given land, milch cows, goats, and shops in market places. This will be through subsidized loan. Someone who fails to elude poverty through these activities will be given scope to work with daily wages paid by the government. Someone who continues to remain poor despite this will be put in jail. (This last jail bit was said perhaps as a joke.)

Bholanath, the half-crazy priest of Shiva temple proclaimed: 'In the coming Shivaratri god Shiva and goddess Parvati will manifest in our village.' (He had gone crazy after reciting the mantra incorrectly over a long period of time during daily worships in a temple.)

The school teacher said: 'Our wattle-and-daub primary school will be promoted to a full high school teaching up to class eleven or at least a minor school teaching up to class seven.'

Chakrapani predicted: 'The courts will be abolished, all court case systems will be replaced by the good old system of five elders or panchayat, and members of appellate panchayat will be selected from every village.'

Nathu Mahalik said: 'The old village will be restored, we will leave the settlement and return to our old village. The dam has eroded and will collapse. All the water has gone out of the dam.'

Penga said: 'Alekh sanyasi will return to the village,'

The former landlord Ramachandra Mangaraj heard everything, knew that these were long winded tittle-tattle, but said nothing. He murmured to himself: 'Oh, they are just exaggerating a little for fun, let them do this.'

Those days, vendors of miscellaneous household goods, vendors of palm wine and hooch, officials promoting deposits in small savings bank run by government post offices, and similar outsiders continued to come to the settlement infrequently because the people still had some money left over from the compensation received for their land taken away for the dam project. Occasionally, a stranger came to the house of Kunti. Suppose a vendor of household goods came near her house, blew his toy trumpet, shook his jangler, a voice emerged from the house like a reflection: 'You charlatans of uncertain parentage, you did not find anyone else to cheat that you have come to me?'

But no one knows what transpired that after some time whenever she heard someone outside, she opened the door. If a vendor was at the lower side of the village, she sent someone there to fetch him. She also called other visitors to the village: officials, fish vendors, bangle makers, people who had come to collect contributions for various purposes, washerwoman (who did not wash clothes, only sprinkled some water on clothes washed after a rite in the clan like birth, death), election officials, police and touts.

She asked everyone: 'Have you brought fig fruits, have you? I need fig fruits?' By then Kunti had become afraid that the person who was due to arrive at the settlement was none else than death. In order to meet death, there is nothing superior to the story of an adult who became a child by seeking shelter of a fig fruit.

But she did not quite know about the strange visitor, who is coming, from whom she had borrowed a thread of promise that has enabled her to live so far. The first to come was only a message: *Listen to me. If I come in the night, they may suspect that I am an armed robber, and rain bullets on me. If I come in daytime, they may think that I am their political opponent and dig away a part of the road. You will stand straight at the spot, make your sari-end long and wave it, bedeck yourself with flowers, because I could be coming.*

This message came written on wind; but in that rocky and dusty settlement there was so little clear air that Kunti breathed in all the clear air and this cleaned her body of the last specks of what she believed was impure.

A day or two after the message came, sudden thunder and thin silvery strings of cloud, which does not bother a traditional farmer, came. When a light rain came and fell like paddy husks, and people shouted *hey, rain has come,* and took into their houses the clothes drying and cattle grazing outside, left their odd jobs and watched the drizzle, then it was a wonder. There was no rain of water, flowers were raining.

Then came a torrential rain of water, loud rains with thunder and lightning. Those who had gone to marketplace could not return to their houses in time though they tried everything possible. The clouds, rain, wind and flowers tore away the indifferent depressiveness of the village. The members in the houses of people who had not returned carried glass covered kerosene lanterns and open kerosene lamps, went to other houses and asked: 'Has your Dasia returned? O mother of Chandra, has your son come back? Dear tearful Sakei, where is your husband?'

These questions amplified the terror of the rains.

'Shut the door of the cowshed.'

'The paddy straw stacks has been opened to dry, they are getting wet, cover this with large grass mats.'

'Do not throw the ash from the hearth there, it is windy, it may flare up a speck of fire in the ash.'

The rain, like the Goddess of Cholera, picks up everything on its way. Somehow Sania's mother escaped from being swept away, though the wind churned her jute sack and widow's white dhoti.

By then, Kunti had become ancient by about one generation. Her days were like huge enormous forests engulfed by fire, and when she lay on her bed to sleep to escape the fire, her sleep disintegrated and blew away like dust in the wind. The stubborn night squatted shamelessly. Time lingered and did not move much. She fell asleep for half of the night and the other half she spent in endless dreams following one after another. The summer nights passed somehow with the fan, crowded festivals and moonlight when there is a moon; but how did she spend these raining nights? Those days, she did not think of anyone. When rains started, she thought of her brother Gobara for a moment and wondered: 'Is there any night in Assam? Or, does it have mornings of blue light for six months in a year and evenings of blue light for the other six months?' Except for this one occasion, she had not thought of anyone else.

After it had rained for seven days, the crudity of rocks near the abode of Village Goddess was washed away, and little plants of flowers and fruits appeared in their crevices. In the rains, the plants swooned as they came up with imperceptible laziness as if they were dancing slowly as they came up. On one of those days, Kunti had picked up from the abode of the Goddess Rangoon Jasmines, *kadamba*, moonbeam, marigold and other flowers and was returning. Light from lightning in the sky shone over her head, but everyone knew so well of her complete banishment that though she was carrying basketfuls of flowers, no one, not even old woman Dhusi who was jabbering with three children on her veranda saw her.

Old woman Dhusi was asking a five-year-old boy, who was her grandson by clan relationship: 'Hey, will you give birth to a child?'

The boy answered: 'No, my mother will.'

'And your wife?'

Before the boy could answer there was loud thunder and lightning and everyone went into the house. The children quarrelled to suckle the old woman's nipples. The most unreasonable and persistent was the five-year-old child who put both the breasts of Dhusi into his mouth.

Dhusi said: 'So you only have a soul, body, desire, hunger and these children do not have those? Everyone has the same soul, and you think they have different souls?'

That night a palanquin of flowers with four beams to carry it descended in the courtyard of Kunti, and flowers rained from the sky. Then there was heavy rain of water. Those from whose houses people had gone out and had not returned in the rains came out of their houses thinking that their people had returned, and heard the sounds of a worship going on and conch shells blowing. (Chandrabhanu, who always boasted that he had gone to meet a minister or the chief minister, had not been able to return. After many days he revealed that he could not return because he was busy arranging relief materials for the people affected by floods.) But perhaps the rains had destroyed a lot of their moral strength. They did not cross the steps of their houses to be soaked with the rain nor went to the place where the worship was held; they did not want to see anything.

In the rain, the flower trees and plants were laden in exuberant reds and yellows. But no one had any idea how much it rained. Even the rain measuring equipment located several kilometres away overflowed everyday there was rainfall, and eventually the equipment was washed away. Of course, after that day the rain measuring equipment did not overflow. All the houses built by government became soggy and drenched. (In fact, the roofs of the housed leaked so much that it poured inside the house when it rained outside, and the people left the houses, quickly put up bamboo-and-leaf huts and stayed there; but I will not say all this. Because you will think that I am hinting at the corruption of Civil Engineering Department. My job is to tell you a fairy tale; why should I get into these troublesome happenings?)

The steel electric poles and their aluminum cables shone like silver though no current passed through them. But the rains had driven the people crazy, they sold off the poles and cables thinking that these were made of silver, and decided to blame the rains for the loss in their reports. Telephones could not be used because the receivers were stuck on the cradles and could not be lifted. From time to time, all kinds of vehicles moving on the roads sank into the soil and disappeared.

The voices of radio and the scenes of television were stuck in the heavy clouds. The letters and newspapers which came to the settlement became wet and thick like the film on hot gruel that was poured out after rice was cooked. The cattle of the village preferred only green fodder and there was plenty of moss, fern and grass, and the cattle did not even smell the letters and newspapers because they were not green. The people did not know what to do with the letters and newspapers.

Like many times before, some villagers ordained with authority that the final end of the universe has come. But very few trusted them, because when it rained for just twenty-four hours these gloomy forecasters said that the end of the universe has come.

When it continued to rain, and Ankamara irrigation project breached and was washed away at many places, and many people, who had fertile land downstream, came up near the settlement and attempted to force their entry into the settlement, Mahadev Mahalinga whose house was at the entrance was watching the rains and reminiscing the times when he had just been married. When he saw the intruders he shouted: 'Go back you selfish plain folks! Our villagers, come out of your houses and push back these land looters.'

Most of the young men who had gone out to work had not returned because of the rains. A child staying with his grandmother ran out of their house and shouted: 'A thousand years ago you had driven us out of the plains and sent us up to the hills of Ankamara village. Now, a thousand years later, you sent us up from Ankamara to this barren rocky mountain. Now what do you want? What are you after? There is nothing here. Get out of here.'

The child picked up a little stone to throw at the intruders... *look, there was a plant under the little stone.*

Right before everyone, the tree grew. After the child had picked up the stone there was a rumble in the hills behind the village which slowly became louder, and bigger stones and rocks rolled down with thundering sound. The cascade of rocks drove away the plains people who had come to occupy the settlement. Below every rock, there was a tree, and the whole settlement was filled up with green trees. Right before the eyes of the people, the canopies of trees grew to touch each other, and became like huge umbrellas.

There, Kunti was gathering flowers everyday and

played with them. The day the trees covered the settlement like an umbrella, and a single drop of rain did not fall on the ground, she divided the flowers into two heaps. She made a garland with one heap. She also put into the garland freshly sprouted leaves of mango, gods' tree and oleander which had been blown in by the air. She wore the garland. The Ayurveda doctor had gone to every house to check the health of the people. He went inside Kunti's house, came out and announced from her veranda: '*Vata*, severe *vata*.'

The doctor explained that *vata* is one type of body condition where air and space are dominant. The person is creative, kind hearted, forgetful. This also causes accumulation of fluid. But the people who heard him understood only the last part and examined their hands and legs.

Kunti slept in the palanquin of flowers. The flowers were absolutely fresh in spite of or maybe because of the rains. She spread the second heap of flowers on her. That is when the Ayurveda doctor came and declared at the small platform (which was meant to hold meetings, but meetings were rarely held): '*Pitta*, severe *pitta*.'

The doctor continued that *pitta* is a combination of fire and water. *Pitta* people have burning sensation in their digestive system, they get irritated easily, and dislike argument. People in the settlement were more familiar with this trait and their heads cooled down.

Because of the canopy of trees, it did not rain much in the village, but the water of previous rains took many days to be drained off. From the straw roof of Nefidi's mother, not one or two but twenty-two pumpkins and pitcher-gourds descended, swam in the water, and entered the house of the daughter of her enemy for seven generations from her father's side, who was also married in Ankamara. A part of the soaked wall between the bed room and the cowshed fell on the leg of Madha Rout (His son is a magistrate in the town and people say that the son has built a big house in a town) from lower street, his leg bone was broken, and then all his arrogance and hubris about his son was broken to smithereens.

Penga's sister, whose legs had slipped before the rains, was nearing the time of childbirth and had earned the honour of daughter-in-law of the moneylender's household, swept the floor with a broom, washed dishes, and since fuel wood was scarce due to the rains, dried wet leaves on her bed of reed mat and slept on the bare ground on a veranda.

The dense trees did not let in much sunlight and it remained darkish even at noon time. When someone grumbled about it, Chakrapani whose profession was to show hurricane lanterns in a country of people who could not see, said: 'This is how our people are. They will not tolerate even a little occasional inconvenience.'

No one sent any information or complaint to the people in government. Besides, why blame the government people? They are low paid, their government accommodations small, inconvenient and without air-conditioning. The politicians look upon every case where relief material did not reach as a political conspiracy, and are always unhappy over this. And in particular, the election to local self governments is due now, which will give legitimate seats of power and opportunities to the unemployed people to make money beyond the legal limits, and after attending to these complex and nonexistent problems, who has the time to attend to the calamities of villagers? If anyone from the settlement had gone to present a grievance before the government people, then it would have given a bad name to every villager that they were rabble-rousers, litigants and touts.

The flow of water subsided slowly in due course, and a confidence returned to the settlement that this will survive. Meanwhile, many people had returned to the village by rowing boats against the current. The heavy rains also showed that many houses had burnt so well under the blazing sun for so many years that the rains could not damage these. When the rains almost stopped, the people got together and cleaned most of bushes from the main road of the village. This was a praiseworthy exercise because otherwise the people of government and other ladies and gentlemen who visited the village would have carried a poor opinion of the villagers that they were uncivilized and wild.

When these things were happening, people remained in a state of euphoric turbulence and had forgotten about Kunti. Before the rains stopped, she received news through the rain that someone is coming who will rescue her from life; though the news came several times and no one had arrived. Here she was becoming imperceptibly smaller, her sari became so big that it twined around her body and often she tripped over it. If the arrival of the promised person had been delayed any more, Kunti would have progressively become diminutive and probably vanished altogether because once the nature has decided unequivocally and firmly to wake up from slumber, what can an ordinary person do?

While waiting for that saviour from life, Kunti thought that this will be her last breath, but it was not to be.

She brushed off the last particle of dust from her sari, as if this last relationship between her and a particle of dust on earth is preventing her from being saved. When the village became forested like before, when it was not possible to distinguish the settlement from Ankamara and deer were jumping in the village and in the night the growl of tiger could be heard, no one noticed that a deer was running to the house of Kunti in the forested darkness. If someone would have observed the deer carefully, he would have seen the fatigue of running for a long distance, the smile of someone who knew many secrets and the restrain of someone who knew what he was doing. When the deer reached the house of Kunti she looked like a little girl, and her body was wrapped so thoroughly that even her palms and feet were not visible. She had two wings grown from her shoulder near the beginning of her arms. She did not wait any longer. As soon as she sat on the deer it ran into the forest and ran deeper into the forest. Sunset was about to come.

Next day when the Ayurveda doctor reached the house of Kunti expecting some decent fee, Kunti was not there.

After hearing the news, a little child asked: 'Did the deer take Kunti away because she had no one else of her own?'

This question perturbed me. Indeed, why did that deer take away Kunti? But then, which other option did I have? How would Kunti go? Since her pension money did not come regularly and since her savings in the government post office had been misappropriated by someone through fraud, would she have died of hunger and thirst? Or, because she did not have anyone to get some essential foods and medicines from the marketplace in town? Or because she did not have anyone to repair her house, it gets washed away in the flood with her? Or she would have died of cold and loneliness or shrunk to death in the incessant rains? Or she would have been soaked and slopped with illness and neglect? No, such denouements are not possible in fairy tales.

Besides who died in the village? No life was like a leaking conch shell that does not emanate the auspicious and exhorting sound when blown with mouth. No one died in the village. The souls of people came at birth and left with death. Only the soul of Kunti did not have to come back because she had been released from the cycle of life and death.

Here my tale ends,

Even as I have said it well,

The flowering plant has met it's end.

Black Eagle Books

www.blackeaglebooks.org
info@blackeaglebooks.org

Black Eagle Books, an independent publisher, was founded
as a nonprofit organization in April, 2019. It is our mission
to connect and engage the Indian diaspora and the world at
large with the best of works of world literature published on
a collaborative platform, with special emphasis on
foregrounding Contemporary Classics and New Writing.